ALIEN ABDUCTION FOR BEGINNERS

THE INTERGALACTIC GUIDE TO HUMANS
BOOK 1

SKYE MACKINNON

Cover by Peryton Covers.

Published by Peryton Press.

skyemackinnon.com

ALIEN ABDUCTION
for beginners

CONTENTS

LESSON 1

INTRODUCTION TO ABDUCTIONS

XIL

This had been a mistake. A big one. Judging from their groans, Havel and Matar thought the same thing. When I'd signed us up for this course, I hadn't expected there to be assignments, let alone exams. It was supposed to be a bit of fun, not an entire degree.

"Is it refundable?" Matar asked with an irritated flick of his tail.

I studied the terms and conditions. Klat. No such luck. And we'd paid way too many credits to just give up before we'd even started.

I grit my teeth. "We're going to do this. Exams be damned. We don't even have to do well in them. There are some planets that accept abductors without qualifications."

Havel flashed his fangs in annoyance. "We know. And look how that's worked out. We're the laughingstock of the entire galaxy."

"Just this sector," I quipped. "And we can still change that. We just need to get it right the one time and everything will be forgotten."

Matar groaned again. "We've tried six times. I can still see the last female waving at us as she stole our escape pod. Do you really think we'll be successful after taking this course?"

"The Intergalactic University has an excellent

reputation. Their classes must be good. And if we fail, we can always choose a different path. I hear space pirating pays quite nicely."

"Kardarians don't become *pirates,*" Havel spat. "They abduct females. It's what we do. What our people have done ever since they discovered spaceflight. We have to do this. There's no other way."

"Yeah, I don't plan on staying a bachelor forever." Matar licked his lips. "I can't wait to have a female of my own. Soft and succulent, ready to worship me."

Havel snickered. "I think you got something wrong there. You're supposed to worship the female, not the other way round. Make her feel like the only woman in the universe. Even I know that. Maybe it's good that we're doing this course after all."

I left them to their bickering and select the first lecture. We were on autopilot and wouldn't get to Kepler Two for another seven intergalactic hours, so we had got time on our hands. I threw it at our main screen, hiding the view of the Scorpion Nebula flying past.

"Now?" Havel groaned. "Don't we have better things to do?"

I shot him a glare. "It was you she ran away from. Sit down and watch this klatting lecture."

He grovelled but both him and Matar took their seats. I was already in my captain's chair. The only difference between my seat and theirs was that mine was a little elevated, giving me a better view of the bridge. It wasn't any comfier and the thick skin on my arse told of the many hours I'd spent in this chair. Autopilot was all well and good, but I was a traditionalist at heart and liked to fly Jade, my ship, manually.

After the logo of the Intergalactic University vanished, a Karangi female appeared on the screen. The third eye on her forehead sparkled with enthusiasm as she introduced herself as Professor Katila welcomed us as her new students. Not that she was actually aware of us. This was a recorded lecture, just like all of them. We'd only get to talk to our professors face to face in seminars and in preparation for our exams. I shuddered. I hated exams.

"Abductions are one of the galaxy's most sacred traditions," she said in her smooth, delicate voice. They'd done well to choose a Karangi to hold these lectures. They were known for their intelligence and benevolence. If a Karangi was able to do an abduction despite their deeply ingrained morals, anyone could.

"Ever since the first species discovered space flight, abductions of lesser beings have taken place. It's a universal urge that cannot be ignored. Whether it's for companionship, research or simply to get a new pet, abductions are your cheap and easy way to get what you need. The rules of the University require me to say at this point that we do not condone slavery in any shape or form."

She smiled, all three eyes full of warmth. I almost felt loved simply by looking at the video of her. "We shall begin this course with the four Ls. Learn. Locate. Lure. Leave."

The four words appeared on the screen. Matar snorted. "She left indeed."

"I don't think that's what Professor Katila meant," I whispered before realising I didn't need to keep my voice down.

"We're currently at the learning stage. You need to know everything you can about how best to abduct. It's not enough to simply know how to take someone from their planet. You have to be prepared for the aftermath."

Matar chuckled again but both Havel and I ignored him.

"Once you've completed the basic modules of this course, you can start thinking about locating your target. There is a lot to consider even if you already know the species and planet you prefer. Knowledge is key for a successful abduction. As soon as you've done your research and have set your eyes on your target, it's time for the luring stage. Some might simply use a tractor beam to get their target aboard, but in my opinion, that lacks finesse. Abducting is an art form and it should be treated as such."

"She's a little over the top, right?" I asked the guys. "How is it art?"

"Maybe that's where we've gone wrong," Havel muttered.

"Finally, leaving the planet. This isn't just a physical task. Your target will feel lost and alone so far from their home. It's your responsibility to make them comfortable and prepare them for their new life. Even if that life means being probed and researched until they expire."

Interesting. Katila was against slavery but didn't mind subjects being experimented on. I didn't know much about probing, but I was pretty certain that it didn't always happen with the consent of the being on the lab table. I supposed we'd cover that later in the course.

"Today, we shall talk about the motivations for your planned abduction," the Professor continued. "You can do this as a solo or group project, although we do recommend beginners to cooperate with other students for their first abduction. It will help you achieve the top grades possible while also assuring a safe and rewarding experience."

A set of questions appeared on the screen, all of them ridiculous. I regretted signing up for this class even more now. Group work. I hated it. I'd never been much of a team player. The raisers in the hatchery had despaired over my desire to sit in a corner on my own, tinkering with some project I'd come across. I only worked with Matar and Havel because they were good friends and excellent at their jobs. Unless it came to abductions. That's where all three of us sucked. Hence this klatting course.

"Do we write down our answers?" Havel asked. "Do we need to submit them?"

"This project is not graded," the Professor's voice replied immediately. It had to be an automatic, recorded message. "But we would like you to send us your answers anyway. My assistants and I will be happy to help you and provide feedback."

Matar rolled his eyes. "Great. Yet more work. I've still got the booster engine to fix. Does this really take priority?"

"Do you want to get our reputation back or not?!" I snapped. "We need to abduct a female and quickly. If this is the only way to achieve that, so be it. The engine can wait until we're done with the first module."

I flicked open my wrist communicator and projected a large piece of virtual paper in front of me. Real paper was way too expensive to use for something like this. I synced it with the guys' comms so that whatever one of us wrote would appear on everyone's paper. It was a great way to avoid having to sit in a circle.

1) Why do you want to conduct an abduction?

"It's part of our culture," Matar said and his words appeared on the paper. "If we don't get this right, we'll be laughed at for the rest of our lives."

"Without respect, we won't get good tariffs on our products," Havel added. "And we need the money."

I sighed. "My father will never let me inherit his wealth unless I can prove to him that I'm not useless and an embarrassment to our species."

Havel snickered. "You don't have to rub it in, we know your family's loaded. Once he dies, you'll be able to buy an entire fleet of ships, not just this one."

As much as I hated my father, I didn't want him to die. I didn't respond to Havel's comment and took a look at the second question instead.

2) How do you imagine your perfect abduction target?

"Soft, beautiful, female, sexy, willing," Havel said with enthusiasm, the words blending into each other. "Fertile. And compatible with our physiology."

Matar laughed. "Don't worry, she doesn't need much to be *compatible* with your tiny cock."

Havel snarled, flashing his fangs. "If you don't watch your tongue, I'm going to make sure to add something poisonous to your next vaccination. How do boils around your balls sound?"

"Cut it, you two," I growled. "Of course we're going to take our target from a species that's similar to our own. We want a mate, not a servant, and certainly not a lab rat."

"And a breeder." Havel smiled. "Can you imagine, us becoming fathers?"

No, I couldn't. None of us was ready for that kind of responsibility. I was sure he knew that, but for now, I'd leave him to his fantasy.

"Clever, funny, courageous," I added to the list.

My friends rolled their eyes but I ignored them. It wasn't all about looks. Especially because I wasn't the most desirable Kardarian that had ever lived. Havel and Matar were lucky, their colouring was what Kardarian females wanted. Deep blues and greens, while I'd been born yellow, the colour of my disgraced great-grandfather. It had only added to the disappointment my father felt whenever he looked at me. I bet that he'd pushed me out of the family long ago if I hadn't been his only child. My mother and he had tried again and again, but I was the only result of their union. They despised me for it.

3) What will you do with your abductee? Will you keep them permanently?

Yes, all three of us wrote as one. I smiled. We'd been unsuccessful so far, which meant that we'd never let our female go once we'd finally captured her. She was going to be ours for the rest of our lives.

"She'll be our mate," I said and the words

appeared below the three Yeses. "Our companion. Our friend. And eventually, the mother to our offspring." I shot a look at Havel. "Mother sounds better than breeder."

He nodded. "Right. Unless she prefers to be called our breeder. Depending on her species, that may be the correct term."

I checked the screen and realised with relief that we'd answered the final question. I quickly compiled our replies and submitted them to Professor Katila. We'd have to wait for her to send us the next lecture, but the university had provided us with several textbooks on abductions. I forwarded them to the others. It was time to do some hardcore reading.

LESSON 2

PREPARE OR FAIL

I stared at the galaxy map, my tail twitching with nervosity. I wrapped it around my leg to keep it out of the way. The other guys were used to it by now, rarely stepping on it, but I'd been self-conscious of it all my life.

Four planets were blinking fast, giving us our possible destinations. The Intergalactic University had sent us a database of abduction-ready planets this morning and now we were trying to find the perfect one.

"What's the green one?" I asked, pointing at the largest dot.

Xil checked the database entry on his comms. "Laranus. Sparsely inhabited. Females are compatible with us but...oh."

"What?"

"They don't have breasts."

I gaped at him. "No breasts? How do they feed their offspring?"

He scrolled through the information, then started to laugh. "They have tubes extending from their pussy that the younglings feed on for several years. Like straws. I doubt the females would be agreeable to sex during that time. It might squash the tubes."

I cringed at the thought of plunging into a female while weird fleshy bits were hanging out of her. No thanks. I wasn't speciest, but that was a little too exotic.

"The red planet is Riva Four," Havel muttered, checking his own comms. "They're very underdeveloped. No spaceflight yet. They still use animals for transportation. I suppose it might make it easier to abduct a female from there. They may even see us as gods. Wouldn't that be fun, being worshipped as a deity? Yes, you can suck my godly cock and receive my holy seed."

I elbowed him. "Don't talk like that. Females don't like vulgar language."

"Who says that?"

"I read it in one of the books," I admitted. "I was bored last night."

"Teacher's pet," Havel snickered. "Did it say anything else that might come in handy?"

I nodded. "Lots. But why would I tell you? I'll use my new knowledge to make our female love me the most."

Havel flashed his fangs at me. Most of our kind had lost them in the process of evolution, but some of us still had the features that told of our predatory heritage. Havel complained about them all the time, saying they got in the way while eating, but he'd refused any offers from dentists to have them filed down. I thought that secretly, he was quite fond of them.

"That one," Xil said and pointed at a blue planet

at the very edge of the galaxy. "Peritus, but the natives call it Earth in most of their languages, not sure why. It seems to have several oceans, but maybe they worship the ground they live on? Maybe they're scared of the water."

"Do they have vaginal tubes?" I asked with trepidation.

"Not that I can see. And they have breasts of all sizes. Some are almost udders. Wow. Imagine burying your head between them, like soft pillows."

Havel laughed. "I'd bury something else between them."

"They only have one truly sentient species on their planet called humans. They've discovered spaceflight and are slowly spreading across the galaxy."

I dimly remembered coming across their kind before. It had to have been on some space station, but all I could recall was the name of their species, nothing more.

"Do they have tails?" I asked carefully.

Xil shot me a knowing look. "No, not that I can see. No fangs, either, but they do have beautiful manes." His eyes widened. "And fur in other places. I like it."

I couldn't resist any longer. I opened my own comms and searched for the IGU's database entry on humans. Several images appeared before my eyes. I was the only one of us who had the implant that connected my comms to my optic nerve. It was handy for looking at information that I didn't want anyone else to see. And porn.

I ignored the image of a male and scrolled to one of a female. She had a long, black mane full of curls, dark skin that reminded me of the pap tree beans we had at home, and yes, there was hair under her arms, between her legs and on her lower legs. Beautiful. My mouth watered. I could get used to having one like her around.

I quickly skimmed the section on human biology. They were compatible with us physically, although there was no information on successful breeding between our species. That worried me a little. Had nobody abducted a human before? Unlikely. The planet was part of the university's database, which meant it had been studied by scientists.

Still, I liked the look of these humans. So much so that I didn't even feel the need to explore the fourth blinking planet on the map.

"How long until we get there?" Havel asked. He seemed just as eager as me to get there quickly."

I frowned. "Two galactic weeks, faster if I get the booster engine sorted. We should have enough fuel for a round trip; no need to stop at a space station on the way."

Xil switched off the holomap and sat back in his captain's chair, a smile curving his ochre lips. "That gives us enough time to complete all the other lectures before we reach the planet. Matar, get that engine fixed as soon as possible. Havel and I can complete the next module without you."

"No way," I protested. "I don't want to miss anything. I'll work on the engine later."

The captain sighed but didn't argue. All of a sudden, the IGU course had become less of a pain in the arse. We needed all the help we could get if we wanted to abduct one of those precious humans.

HUMAN. I let my tongue taste the word. Human. It didn't sound too bad. Not quite as pretty as Kardarian, but that didn't matter. Our female would have her own name. Something beautiful, I was sure of it. If not, we'd give her a new name. Maybe we couldn't even pronounce hers.

"We need to get a translator," I said into the silent room. "Or do we have one on board? I'm not sure she'll speak anything but...whatever humans speak."

"They have hundreds of languages on their planet," Havel said without looking up from the text he was reading. "But it seems all of them have been catalogued, so a standard interstellar translating device will work. I think we have a couple of them in the med bay, they came with the Jade. I'll check later."

I nodded and got back to reading the chapter

about Earth's geography that I'd just started before I got distracted once again. I didn't think I needed to know any of this. We weren't planning to settle on our abductee's planet. We'd land, find a suitable female, abduct her, and leave. I couldn't care less how many continents they had, but Professor Katila said there would be a test, so it was better to be prepared. Failing wasn't an option.

Four continents. There had been another, but it had disappeared when ocean levels rose. Humans seemed to be a very destructive species. They'd almost torn their planet to pieces before just about managing to turn it around, becoming more aware of the environment they depended on. Still, I understood why they'd started exploring the stars. It didn't look like a planet I'd like to live on. Pollution was ripe. I flicked forward a few pages until I found information about air quality. Thank A'Ta, we'd be able to breathe their air.

"Look at those breasts," Xil groaned and sent a picture to all our comms.

I sucked in a breath when the naked female appeared in front of my eyes, projected into my optic nerve. She was hot. Scorching hot. Her breasts were full and tempted me to reach out and squeeze them. She had strange rubbery shafts in their centre, probably to let the milk flow into her offspring's mouth. Kardarian breasts didn't have those, they had pores through which the milk diffused into the open.

What would it feel like to suck on those fleshy knobs?

"What do you call those...appendages?" Havel asked breathlessly.

"Nipples," Xil answered, his face turning slightly orange. He was aroused. And not just him. My cocks strained against my uniform bottoms. How could an alien female make me feel this turned on? It was just a 3D image, nothing more. This wasn't our abductee and I shouldn't feel this way about a random female.

I pushed the image away together with the boring text about geography. "Let's listen to her lecture," I proposed. "We can continue reading tonight once we've done our other tasks."

Our captain nodded and turned on the main screen, touching his comms until Professor Katila appeared in front of us. Her third eye blinked a couple of times while her other two eyes stayed wide open.

"Welcome to our second lecture," she said with a wide smile. "Today we are talking about how to prepare for an abduction. If you've looked at the recommended reading, you'll see that there's a lot of ground to cover. If you don't prepare, you will fail. Some of you may have already tried your first abduction. If you're taking this course, I assume it didn't go well."

"You could say that," I scoffed. "Not at all."

"Preparation is key. Remember the four Ls. Learn

and Locate are far more important than Lure and Leave. Without the first step, you will fail at the subsequent three." She smiled again, some of her seriousness washing away. "If you haven't decided on a planet and species yet, now is the time. Once you have, please watch the next part of this lecture."

She froze for a moment until Xil pressed the play button again and the recording resumed.

"Now that you have decided on a species, it's time to do as much research as you can manage. If you're working as a group, you can split up these topics, but I do recommend that all of you learn the basics. Remember, it is your duty to care for your abductee. They will have to get the right food, the right sleeping arrangements, even medical care."

"I'll do her medical care," Havel interrupted. "And I'll do any necessary probing too."

Xil shushed him so we could continue listening to the professor talking.

"You will also have to know about the planet's defences. Some species don't take kindly to having members of their own abducted, while others may even pay you to take some of their undesirables. Either way, you need to make sure that you won't be shot down or pursued by their military. This is why we often recommend planets with no space-faring capabilities for abduction beginners."

"Too late," I muttered. "We're definitely getting a human."

"A human with breasts," Havel reiterated. "Big ones."

"I will send you all a list of areas to research. Since all of you are likely focusing on a different planet, you don't need to send me your results, but please contact me if you have any questions or can't find enough material about a particular species."

Her lecture was followed by the logo of the IGU, a strange animal that I'd never been able to identify. It had to be from a planet I'd not been to yet.

"Let's split the list in three," Xil said, already sending Havel and me our parts. "Research your topics and then we'll get together tomorrow and share our results. Put anything that everyone should know into a separate document, that way we can compile a guide to our future human."

I scanned the list he'd sent me. Food. Technology. A few other things that aligned with my interests. I shot Xil an appreciative look and left the room, still thinking about breasts.

IT TURNED out that humans ate a lot of strange things. Most of the animals they ate didn't mean anything to me, but it would be hard to replicate those. We had a food replicator, of course, but it needed blueprints and ingredients for anything we wanted it to make. We'd fed it the genetic code of the livestock we were used to from our home planet, but we couldn't exactly probe every single Earth animal just on the off-chance that our female might like their meat. Many of the vegetables humans ate weren't too different from what we were used to, especially the various kinds of roots they grew in the ground. Again, a connection to the earth. I hadn't found any explanation for their planet's strange name yet, but their religions weren't on my list. Maybe one of the others would discover the answer.

They drank something called water, which was the base of most of their drinks. A fairly simple mix of hydrogen and oxygen. Hydrogen wasn't a common element in this part of the galaxy, but we could easily synthesise it to make that drink for her.

After I read through everything I could find on their various dishes - very confusing since every single tiny village had their own foods, which meant we'd never be able to know what our abductee liked until we knew where she came from - I continued on to exploring Earth's technological advances. They were about five hundred rotations behind Kardar, with their spacefaring technology still in its infancy. Humans seemed excellent at exploiting other species' technology though, which meant they had access to spacecraft that they hadn't developed themselves. Cheeky. They were scavengers, in a way. Not unlike the three of us. We called ourselves traders, but we got a lot of our goods by entering abandoned space stations and crashed ships.

Earth's defences were negligible, at least the tech they'd created on their own. Without knowing whose technology they may have borrowed, we would have to be careful, just in case. If they'd got their hands on Lurian weaponry, we'd never leave the planet in one piece.

I made a note to take enough weapons with us to the surface. We wouldn't use them on our female, of course, but on anyone who would try to stop us. We deserved a female and we would take her no matter how much resistance we had to fight against. All three of us had served in the Kardar military, although as a healer, Havel hadn't been on the front lines. His fighting skills were rudimentary at best, but Xil made up for that. He could have risen high in the military if he hadn't decided to leave with us.

I blinked, tiredness making itself known. I still had to fix that booster engine. I sighed, but then remembered that the faster I fixed it, the quicker we'd get to our female and her voluptuous breasts. I grinned at the thought. Yes, I could get used to seeing a female like that every single day until the end of my life.

LESSON 3

HOW TO CHOOSE THE RIGHT FEMALE

HAVEL

Earth looked rather pretty from space. Its atmosphere cloaked it in a blue sheen, a similar colour to the oceans below. We'd taken our position in orbit, ready to take the shuttle to the surface. The tractor beam wasn't strong enough to cover this distance, and besides, I always loved travelling on the shuttle. Steering it through space was exhilarating.

"What are you going to wear?" Matar asked, looking uncharacteristically insecure. He wouldn't usually care what other people thought of him, but he did seem to care about our female. To be fair, I felt the same. I wanted to impress her. Show off the muscles I'd worked so hard to achieve. I wasn't a warrior, not like Xil and Matar, but that didn't mean I didn't have abs to die for. That's what my ex had said, anyway, before complaining that she didn't find the rest of me to die for. I'd show our human that I was irresistible. She'd fall in love with me.

"We're going to have to use disguises," Xil interrupted before I could reply. "We don't know what humans' reactions to us will be. We don't want to stand out and attract unwarranted attention. Our abductee might flee if she sees how different we are from her."

I sighed. "I don't like those holosuits. They're itchy."

"You'll wear yours," the captain snapped. "And if you complain again, I'll make sure you look as ugly as the Black Oboto himself."

I flashed my fangs at him but didn't protest. He was right. The holosuits would make us appear human, letting us blend in.

"I'll download some templates," I sighed and opened the holosuit catalogue on my comm. They didn't have a lot of choice when it came to human costumes, but I quickly chose the three best looking ones. Mine was the one most similar to the sexy big-boobed female we'd seen on the photograph. Dark skin, long black hair that was braided in a strange but fascinating way, and an outfit that left little to the imagination. His dark green shirt was open, revealing his smooth chest. I ran my tongue along my fangs like I always did when I was confused. His skin was so...bare. No scales, no spots, not even tribal tattoos. How very boring.

My own torso was covered in dark spots that resembled the Earth leopard I'd read about during my research. It was a leftover from our evolution, a camouflage feature that wasn't of any use to me now. Still, I loved my spots. They were nice and smooth to touch, unlike Xil's scales. I hoped our female would like us despite all our differences.

"Before we get dressed, we need to decide on

where to land," Xil said. "We've agreed on what kind of female we want to abduct, but someone like her could be anywhere on that planet. There are billions of humans crawling in their precious earth and we need to figure out how to find *the one*."

"Maybe we should ask the Professor," I suggested. "She keeps saying that she wants us to get in touch if we have questions. It might make a good impression on her if we ask for advice."

"Or it might make us look like idiots," Matar muttered darkly. "I say we should simply choose a continent at random and let A'Ta's divine tail guide us."

I sighed. "You're the only one here who believes in A'Ta. I'd much prefer our research to guide us. Or our teacher."

"We shall call her," Xil said in his best captain's voice. He always sounded older when he did that. It was hard to resist a command given in that dominant tone and he took advantage of that whenever he needed to.

Before Matar could protest again, Xil had already opened a communication channel to the IGU. Their logo appeared on the screen, followed by a hairy furball with tentacles instead of arms. A dentril, a rare and exotic species. I'd never met one in person. It was said that their fur was poisonous to the touch and their cuteness a natural weapon.

"State your business," the dentril squeaked. I had to suppress a grin. It was adorable.

"We'd like to speak with Professor Katila. We're her students."

The creature's tiny orange eyes blinked a couple of times, as if it found that unlikely. He was right, the three of us looked more like space pirates than intellectuals.

"I shall connect you," it said after a while and the IGU logo appeared once again. One day I'd find out what animal they'd adopted as their mascot. There had to be a reason for it.

A tired-looking Professor Katila flashed into view. Her third eye was closed as if part of her was sleeping. Curious. I'd never had the chance to study Karangi physiology in detail, but I was sure it was fascinating.

"How can I help you?" she asked, clearly suppressing a yawn. None of us had checked what time it was on the IGU station, so we may well have woken her from her sleep. Not exactly the best way to make a good impression on the person who'd grade us at the end of our course.

"Professor, we're about to land on the planet we've chosen and we could do with some advice," Xil said politely.

"Which planet?"

"Peritus. Earth."

Her third eye flew open. "Earth. Now that's an

unusual choice. May I ask why you decided on that planet?"

"Boobs," Matar whispered. I cringed, hoping the microphone hadn't picked up his comment. Our Professor was female and I didn't want to offend her. I'd always been ambitious and I wanted to do well in this assignment.

"The females there are compatible with our species and fulfilled all other criteria we'd come up with," Xil said smoothly. "Their lifespan is a little shorter but the advantages of a match with a human outweigh the differences."

Her third eye blinked while the others stayed open. "None of my students have attempted to abduct a human in a while. They're a strange kind. No physical defences to speak of, but their minds are sharp. They're willing to sacrifice a lot to get what they want."

That matched our research. Humans were weak and yet not.

"Humans exist in various colours, just like you Kardarians, but just like with you, they're all the same on the inside. I'd recommend choosing a female that's not too small unless you don't plan to use her for...physical purposes."

Her third eye twitched with amusement.

"Thank you for the advice," Xil said and bowed his head. "Anything else we should know?"

"It sometimes helps to keep them in only one

room in the beginning until they acclimatise to their new life. They can be both irrational and curious, and you really don't want them running amok around your ship."

I exchanged a look with the others and cringed. Yes, we'd already experienced that with the last female we'd tried to abduct. We'd learned from that. This time, all our escape pods had been biolocked to the three of us. Same with the ship controls and the board computer. The female wouldn't be able to get off this ship unless we let her - which, of course, we wouldn't. She was ours to keep.

"Is there a particular continent we should choose?" Matar asked.

"I'm not an expert on Peritus geography, but as far as I know, it doesn't matter. In the past hundred years or so, their governments have worked hard to make sure everyone on the planet has equal opportunities and resources. However, I assume you have read O'ltg'si's research on socioeconomic influences on abductions?"

I nodded enthusiastically, while the other two pretended to know what she was talking about. I smirked. I'd enjoyed that particular research and thought it might come in handy.

"It can be beneficial to abduct someone from a poor background," Professor Katila summarised the study. "That plus no or very few family ties will make them quicker to adjust to their new life."

"A poor orphan," Xil muttered. "Makes sense."

"How do we identify one, though?" Matar asked the Professor. "I assume they don't run around with 'I am an orphan' signs on Peritus?"

Katila chuckled. "No, they don't. But you could hack into their government databases and find the information that way. Or you simply go to one of the poorer districts in whatever settlement you land and search for an abductee manually. Either way, I wish you the best of luck with your assignment. Document everything as best as you possibly can so that I can give you a good grade."

She smiled and ended the transmission.

I glanced at the guys. "Are we going to do the database thing? I'm sure Matar can hack whatever security measures they use."

Xil shook his head. "I feel like going hunting will be more fun. Plus, it'll give us more material for our assignment reports." He rolled his eyes. "Remember, this isn't just an abduction, it's also a practical exercise for the IGU."

It wasn't hard to forget that, not after having spent the past week reading copious amounts of research papers and listening to virtual lectures. I felt as prepared as I could be. The last few times we'd tried to abduct a female, we hadn't known what we were doing. This time, we were ready.

"Let's randomly choose a place," Matar suggested. "I can let the computer run through all the names of towns and cities on Peritus and have it stop at a random time."

I nodded. "Sounds as good a method as any."

Xil inclined his head in agreement. "Start it. I'll be the one to say stop."

Matar moved his hands in a strange dance; inputting data into his implanted comms device. It always looked strange to us because we couldn't see the interface he saw in front of him. I was glad I hadn't decided to get the same implant. I liked my vision without the influence of others.

"Starting now," he said after a moment.

Xil and I waited, locking eyes. My breathing was growing faster as I realised the significance of this moment. We were finally choosing where to go. Where to find our perfect female. In a few hours, we'd hold her in our arms. She might be riding my cock by the end of the day.

I resisted the urge to touch myself. She'd do that for me, soon.

PRACTICAL ASSIGNMENT

ABDUCTING A HUMAN

TRISH

The heat outside was suffocating. The air inside was even worse. The shack I currently called my home didn't have air conditioning. It didn't even have electricity.

I wiped the sweat off my face, very aware that it would be back within minutes. My body was wet all over. An entire lake was pooling beneath my boobs and I didn't even want to think about my armpits. No deodorant was strong enough for this kind of heat-induced sweating.

It had to be the hottest day of the year. The hottest day in years. I didn't have a thermometer but I didn't need one to know that staying outside for too long would be lethal. Yet I had errands to run and staying home would mean another evening without food to keep the hunger at bay. I had to leave my shack, there was no way around it.

I covered my purple hair beneath a large sun hat and made sure my sunscreen film still covered my skin. I'd stolen it, but it had been worth the guilt. My skin had always been prone to sunburn and this high-tech film prevented it almost entirely. I'd have to recharge it soon, but for that, I needed to find somewhere with an open electricity port. In this town, those were rare. The world may have recovered from the wars and natural catastrophes in most places, but not here. This was a dirt hole that I'd tried to escape ever since my parents had abandoned me. Problem was, leaving was hard if you had no money. So I'd spent the past few years trying to make not only a living but also to put away some savings. And failed. I didn't even have enough money to pay for my dinner today.

Hopefully, Chadra would have some work for me. I adjusted my hat one last time, making sure its wide brim would throw some shade over my eyes - both to protect from the sun as well as unwanted attention - before leaving my shack. I didn't bother locking the door. If someone wanted to break in, they'd be able to do so without much effort. Besides, I had no valuables to steal and I doubted anyone would take the few things I had. They wouldn't bring them any money at the market. Most of it had been found or stolen. I'd become good at repairing broken things so that I could use them nonetheless.

I hurried along the dusty road leading into town. My shack was at the very outskirts, in the slums, although of course, nobody called them that. Slums had existed two centuries ago, but not any longer. No, we weren't supposed to exist. The people in power ignored us and we ignored them in turn. This was a lawless, dangerous place, but it wasn't like I could afford to live anywhere else. I paid exactly zero rent because, well, I lived in a tiny wooden hut with a leaky roof. Not exactly luxury.

The shiny dome of the spaceport at the edge of the desert glinted in the sun. I blinked and looked away before I could start having fantasies yet again, dreams of leaving not just this town, but the entire planet. Those were childish. They were vacancies to work on spaceships, yes, but I had no skills and qualifications that would ever get me there. No, I was destined to stay here, starving, always hoping for a miracle.

Chadra's shop was empty and refreshingly cool. It was a ramshackle store that was filled with all sorts of unnecessary crap, but the owner was kind and often had work for me. I gave two marble statues a questioning look. Not exactly something people in this part of town would buy.

"Those are new." Chadra appeared from behind a curtain, barely managing to squeeze through the doorway. She was big, no, massive. Three of me could have filled her clothes and there would still have been space. Her white hair was braided around her head like a crown, giving her a somewhat pompous appearance, especially when paired with her slightly upturned nose that always made her look arrogant and aloof.

"What are they for?"

She shrugged. "Coat stands? Oversized garden gnomes? I'm sure I'll find a seller eventually. But I doubt that's why you're here."

"Got any jobs for me? I could do with some work."

Chadra rolled her eyes. "You always do. Why don't you try to find a full-time job somewhere? You're a clever girl."

"Woman," I corrected. I barely reached the five-foot mark and people often thought me younger than I was. It was annoying but it also had its advantages. I'd been let off by the police more than once because I got them to believe I was simply a teenager, not yet of age, and therefore not worth the trouble.

"And nobody wants to employ someone like me. I never even finished school."

"Qualifications have nothing to do with intelligence. You're a quick learner. If I could, I'd employ you as my assistant, but I wouldn't be able to afford you. Still, you'll be pleased to hear I've got a job for you. A courier run to the spaceport."

I groaned. That meant I'd have to spend all afternoon in the burning heat.

"Want to say something?" Chandra asked with a smirk.

"No. It's fine. Great. Wonderful. What do you need me to deliver?"

She pulled a small parcel from a drawer, not much bigger than my hand. Jewellery, maybe? It had to be something small yet valuable. Chandra wouldn't have something delivered if it wasn't worth it.

"Don't ask questions, don't look at the customer for too long. Just get to the spaceport as fast as you can and ask for a Mrs Lester."

"Can I get a scooter?" I asked hopefully and to my surprise, Chandra nodded.

"You'd never get there fast enough by foot. But if it gets even the tiniest scratch, I'm going to have to take it off your wages. And because I don't pay you much, it's going to take years for you to repay, so you better don't have an accident."

I gulped, but it wasn't like I had a choice. I needed the money.

Chadra pulled a bundle of keys from her pockets and threw one of them at me. I caught it easily and grabbed it tightly, unable to suppress a grin. I'd not ridden on a scooter in years. This was going to be fun.

Half an hour later, I was on the side of the road, my knees bleeding, the scooter wrecked. And my head hurt like hell. I hadn't worn a helmet because there hadn't been one. Something wet tickled my cheek. Tears? I rubbed my face before looking at my hands. My skin was stained with red. A head wound. Just what I needed.

I let myself fall back onto the hot sand. I didn't have the energy to get up and inspect the damage.

This was it, the moment the last dream turned into dust. I'd have to spend years paying for what just happened, like Chandra warned me. Years of starvation. Instead of improving my life, I was making it worse.

I closed my eyes, unwilling to look at the damaged scooter any longer. I wasn't quite sure what had happened. It had suddenly stopped and I'd been flung through the air, over the handles and onto the hard ground. Everything ached. For some reason, the scooter had then started to drive again, on its own, right into a brick wall that had once been part of a house. Not anymore. The homes that had stood here had all been abandoned when the spaceport had been built five decades ago. Now, they were nothing but ruins.

My head was starting to pound as if someone was banging against it from the inside. I must have got hurt more than I first thought. I couldn't afford to go to a doctor or even call an ambulance, so I just had to wait until it got better.

The sun was quickly drying the blood on my face, turning it into something that felt like a mud mask. A wave of vertigo overcame me even though I was lying in the sand. The ground swayed beneath me and bile rose in my throat. Don't puke. Please don't puke.

The headache was getting worse. Was this the end? Was I going to die in a ditch, alone with no witness but the scorching sun? It would turn my body into a burned crisp before anyone removed my remains.

Even though this was the road to the spaceport, nobody had driven past since my crash. People would start passing by once their shifts ended later today, but now everything was quiet and deserted.

I let my mind drift, unable to stay focused. The pain pulled me away, wrapping me in its arms and telling me not to worry. I welcomed it. There was no point in resisting. Darkness lingered around the edges of my mind, waiting for me. Soon. For now, the pain wasn't ready to let me go quite yet. It explored my body, showing me all the places I'd been hurt in. My legs, my back, my head. I wished for the darkness to swallow me. I didn't want to have to wait. Any delay meant suffering. I'd fought all my life and now I was done fighting. It was time to simply give in to the temptation of everlasting sleep.

A shadow fell over my face, instantly cooling my skin now that it was no longer being grilled by the sun. Someone was talking from high above, several someones. Men. I couldn't make out their words, but I was grateful for the shade they gave me.

I waited for them to leave so that I could die in peace, but they didn't move. Something - no, one of them - touched me by the shoulders. I groaned. I was too tired to move, even opening my eyes seemed like too much of a task.

Cool fingers touched my cheek. Inside, I smiled. Such a nice feeling. It was lovely of them to stay with me while I died. I wouldn't have a funeral but this was even better. I was still alive and knew they were here. Funerals were kind of pointless for the dead person.

More fingers on my face. What were they doing? One of them touched my eyes, gently, ever so softly.

I wanted to see them, I was so curious, but when they pulled up my lids and let me see them, I regretted that.

The sight of a bright blue man with glistening fangs was the sight that finally drove me over the edge and into the waiting embrace of darkness.

LESSON 5

BASIC TECHNIQUES IN DEALING WITH AN ANGRY FEMALE

XIL

This had been our easiest abduction to date. Ironic, since we'd put the most work and resources into it.

We'd found the perfect female without having to spend any time at all on her hot, humid planet. Our randomly chosen location sadly hadn't brought us to lush forests or sparkling oceans. No, it had been a dirty hovel in the middle of nowhere.

"She's healing well," Havel reported. "I'm keeping her sedated though until all her injuries have been dealt with."

I nodded, pleased with how things were turning out. We'd carried her right into our med bay where Havel was now working on her.

She was gorgeous now that Havel had removed the layers of dirt caking her face. Her skin had a reddish sheen in some places but not in others. Maybe they were like my spots, designed for camouflage. In that hot and sandy place, orange and reds would be great to hide in plain sight. She was special, I knew that already. The way her eyes had widened in surprise when she'd seen us made my heart beat faster. She'd seen us as the saviours we were. We'd come to take her away from that place and she was grateful for it, I was sure of it.

"How long until she wakes?" I asked our healer.

"Two hours, maybe three. I want to make sure she's definitely not in pain."

I nodded. "Good. That gives us the chance to check in with the IGU and see if there's a new lecture to watch."

Matar groaned. "Seriously? Now? Can't we just stay here with her? I don't want to leave her, not now that we finally have been successful."

With a sigh, I had a screen descend from the ceiling. "We can watch it here."

I checked the IGU's student dashboard. A large questionnaire waited to be filled in about our abduction, but I clicked on the lecture instead.

Module 5: How to deal with an angry abductee.

I exchanged a look with the others, then let my eyes drift over our sleeping human. I doubted we'd need that lecture. She was going to be grateful that we rescued and healed her. She had no reason to be angry. If everything went well, she'd find ways to show her gratitude. My cock twitched, growing hard. It had been semi-aroused ever since we'd brought her onto our ship. I was aching to plunge into our human's depths to find out what she felt like. There'd be enough time for that though. This was only the beginning.

Professor Katila appeared on the screen. Her

third eye was closed and she had a strangely serene expression as if she'd just emerged from a trance.

"Welcome, students. If you're watching this lecture, I assume that you have successfully abducted a being from another planet. You may think that the hard work is done, but you'd be wrong. The act of abduction is easy. The hard part is yet to come."

I gulped. That didn't sound promising in the slightest.

"Your abductee will be scared, no, terrified. You've ripped them from their home and from everything they've ever known. Depending on what planet you chose, they may have never seen an alien before. You need to be aware of that and proceed slowly."

My cock didn't agree with that statement. Down, boy. You'll get your chance.

"You will have to draw on all the cultural research you've undertaken. If you don't speak their language, fit them with a translator."

"Already done," Havel whispered, clearly pleased with himself.

"Communication is key. Sit them down and patiently explain that you have abducted them. Tell them that there is no way they're going to return to their home planet. It's important to be open with them from the start. They will get over the shock more quickly that way. Introduce yourselves and make sure to answer any questions they may have about your species. If you have any physical features that may be unfamiliar to your abductee, show them at this point. Be open about your differences and highlight the similarities. Once this step is done, tell them what your plan is, whether that's research, companionship or something else entirely."

Her third eye blinked open lazily and she used her slender fingers to wipe the sleep from it.

"If you require help with how to do what I call *the talk*, you can find several pointer sheets in your files. They'll give you helpful conversation starters. As always, you can contact me with questions. Our next lecture will be all about probing, an essential skill for every capable abductor, even if you don't plan to conduct research on your subject. I'll see you then."

The screen turned black. That was a quick lecture. Not that I was complaining. Sometimes Professor Katila droned on and on, giving us more information than I could ever process. Not today.

I looked at our sleeping human. *Ours*. Havel had removed her clothes to access all her wounds, but he'd immediately covered her with a sheet. We'd barely got a look at her body and seeing her full, round breasts push against the fabric from beneath wasn't enough.

"Uncover her," I ordered. "I need to see what we abducted."

"Who," Havel corrected drily but he did as I'd asked.

She was small, much smaller than a Kardarian female would ever be, and didn't have enough flesh on her bones. Was she supposed to be this way or was she emaciated? We'd have to find out once she woke. Her hips were wide and strong, perfect for birthing our offspring. She only had five fingers and toes each, but I'd read that this was the norm for humans. I curled my six fingers into a fist. Maybe Havel could give her those extra digits to make her look a little more normal.

"I love her breasts," Matar sighed in contentment. "Look how they'd fit into my hands."

He got up, but Havel stepped in his way. "No touching until she's awake."

Matar growled, his tail slapping against the floor. "You don't tell me what to do."

"But the Captain does." Havel shot me a stern look.

I wanted to touch her too, but our healer was right, this wasn't the time to explore her body. "Later," I said. "Sit down. It will be more fun when she's awake and can tell us how good it feels."

"Can't you wake her now?" Matar complained. "She looks healthy to me."

Havel rolled his eyes but checked his medical instruments. "In theory, I could. But are we all feeling ready to have *the talk* with her?"

I nodded. "I'll take the lead. Havel, try to keep your fangs hidden for now. Matar, no sudden tail movements. We don't want to scare her."

Both of them inclined their heads in agreement, before Havel started adjusting the machines that were keeping our human unconscious.

"It'll take a few minutes for her to fully wake. Be patient. Let her wake up naturally and take in her surroundings. Maybe we should all move back a little."

The three of us retreated to the back of the room. I didn't want to be that far away from her, but Havel's advice made sense. We had to go slowly or we'd end up in the same situation as last time when our abductee had run around the ship like crazy, threatened us with our own weapons before jumping onto an escape pod. I shook my head to dispel the memory. The embarrassment of that still hurt.

The human moaned softly, but her eyes stayed closed.

"This could take a while," Havel whispered. "I've tried to find out as much about their physiology as possible, but a lot of it is still guesswork."

I shushed him with a glare. She didn't need to hear us talk about her like a lab experiment when she first woke up.

We waited in silence, the tension rising with every minute that passed. Finally, her eyelids twitched and she let out another moan. That sound woke something in me, a feral instinct to protect this female. I clenched my fists to prevent me from storming to her side to hug her to my chest. She was *mine.*

She opened her eyes but didn't sit up yet. All she could see was the ceiling, which was probably the blandest ceiling in the entire ship. Our vessel was old but we made sure to keep it clean and homely. We spent most of the year on the ship and it therefore had to feel like a place we wanted to spend time in. Matar had decorated most of the walls with colourful, abstract paintings. He growled at anyone who commented on them, but I knew he was secretly proud of his art, even though it didn't fit into the image of the macho, growly, aggressive male he tried to be.

The med bay, however, hadn't been painted and was boring shades of grey and white. With a white sheet covering most of her body, her dark hair stood out even more. Kardarian females didn't have manes like that. They had short, wiry tendrils sprouting from their scalp, but nothing as soft and lush as this. I couldn't wait to have tiny Kardarians with long, soft manes on my arm, looking up at their papa with adoration.

"Hello?" she asked, her voice hoarse as if she'd screamed a lot. Maybe it was dehydration.

"Did you give her that oxygen-hydrogen fluid humans like?" I whispered to Havel.

His eyes widened. "I forgot. I made some but I only gave her standard fluids to rehydrate her, not what they call water."

I was tempted to rip off his head, but we needed our healer.

"Get her some right now."

"Shouldn't we wait-"

"What the fuck?" the female suddenly exclaimed and we turned back to her. She'd sat up and was staring at us. Time to follow Professor Katila's instructions and start *the talk.*

"Hello, female," I began, "you have been abducted and are now on the Jade, my ship. You will not return to Earth. You will become our mate and breeder and you will be happy with us. Do you have any questions?"

She blinked several times, then rubbed her eyes. Was there something wrong with her? I shot a panicked look at Havel, but he didn't seem too worried.

I realised I'd forgotten part of my speech and quickly continued. "I am Xil, Captain of this ship. This is Havel, our healer, and Matar, our engineer. We are Kardarians, one of the most powerful species in the galaxy. We are compatible with you, although you may need some practice to accept our cocks because you're so small. We don't know yet if we're compatible for breeding, but we will find out. Oh, and-"

I ripped open my uniform to expose my mottled chest. "I have large spots and scales. Havel has fangs. Matar has a tail. Besides that, we aren't all that different from you. Except that you're missing fingers."

"Very well done," Matar whispered. Havel looked pleased with my speech as well.

The female, however, didn't react as I'd planned. Not at all. She started laughing. She threw her head back and laughed, her entire body shaking from the giggles breaking from her chest.

"Is she reacting to the drugs you gave her?" I asked Havel.

"I doubt it. Maybe it's her way of communicating her happiness at the situation?"

I shrugged. Humans were strange, so this may as well be her showing us how pleased she was with us.

"Do you have any questions, female?" I asked, hoping she'd take the hint and stop laughing.

She gasped for breath in between giggles, causing concern to rise in my chest which turned my scales a darker shade of yellow.

"This is a joke, right?" she asked breathlessly. "Is this my punishment for breaking the scooter? Did Chadra put you up to this?"

Again, the three of us exchanged a look. Chadra? Punishment?

"If you'd like to be punished, we'd be happy to comply," Matar said smoothly. "I've heard some aliens expect punishment when they're abducted. I'd be happy to spank you if you wish."

The female immediately stopped laughing and stared at Matar. "Spank me?"

He held up a hand. "Slap you on your bum."

"I know what spanking is. What the hell? Why are you doing this?"

"It's part of our culture," I explained. "We've wanted to abduct a female for so long and you're just what we were looking for." I didn't tell her that we'd failed many times before. She didn't have to know that. I wanted her to see us as strong, capable males who'd given her the perfect abduction experience.

"Abduction experience," she echoed. "I think the joke is over now. Can I just get my scooter back and leave?"

"You cannot leave," I said as gently as I could. "I already told you that. We're in space and on route to Kardar. You will never return to Earth. We are your mates and this ship is your home."

To my surprise, she snorted. "Yeah, sure. You're great actors, I give you that, although you should work on your script. No aliens would ever talk like that."

"But we are aliens," Havel interrupted. "Here's proof of what the Captain has been saying."

The blinds to our right shot up, revealing a large window. Outside, space was endless and beautiful. I'd always loved looking at the stars, wondering which ones I'd visit in my lifetime. I smiled at the sight, then turned to the female to see her reaction.

Her mouth had fallen open, revealing her very flat teeth. Not a single fang in sight. Havel was the only one of us with pronounced fangs, but even Matar and I had sharp teeth that could rip a piece of flesh off a bone. Yet more proof that humans were incapable of defending themselves.

"That's...it can't be real," the female muttered. She slipped off the bed and walked to the window with slow, unsteady steps. Havel moved to help her, but I held him back. I wanted to see what she'd do next.

She lay her hands against the window as if trying to touch the stars outside. I smiled. She was already starting to understand the beauty of our surroundings.

"This is a simulation," she said, her voice becoming steadier. "I don't know how you're paying for it, but this has gone on long enough. Don't you dare charge me for it. I'm going to have to work years to pay off Chadra's scooter already."

"I don't know what you're talking about, female, but this isn't a simulation," I assured her. "We can have a true simulation at some point so we can show you our planet, but now isn't the time. What is your name?"

I knew I should have asked that earlier, but luckily Professor Katila wasn't here to grade us on our performance. We'd simply tell her that everything went smoothly.

"That's none of your business," the human snapped. "And I'm leaving."

To her detriment, the three of us were standing right in front of the only door leading out of the med bay. And there was no way we'd let her go. Not after the escape pod drama.

"Sit down and ask us questions," I told her and pointed at the bed. "You're supposed to ask about your new life and us."

She raised her eyebrows and I realised they were brown rather than pink. Curious. "I'm *supposed* to?"

Matar nodded enthusiastically. "It's what it says in the manual. You're full of questions and we'll do our best to answer them. It will calm you down and prepare you for the next step."

"What's the next step?" she asked, her voice wavering a little.

Havel grinned, happy to have reached his favourite subject. "Probing."

LESSON 6

PROBING FOR BEGINNERS

HAVEL

She stared at me as if I was the alien. Something to inspect and examine and then put into a display case. I didn't think she'd fully comprehended that this was real. It wasn't a joke and it didn't have anything to do with her scooter. Not that I understood what all that was about. We'd found her next to a crashed vehicle, but I didn't know why anyone would dress up as aliens as a result of that happening. Humans were strange.

"Probing?" she asked in a high-pitched voice.

I nodded, smiling in anticipation of something I'd looked forward to ever since I'd seen the module in the IGU course description.

"It's an important part of any alien abduction," I explained. "Abductees expect to be probed. If you look at human reports of abductions, most of them report probing, so we wouldn't want to disappoint you."

"Disappoint me?" she screeched. I didn't know female voices could go that high. It actually hurt my sensitive ears.

"Exactly. We know you want to be probed and I'll do my best to make it all you've ever imagined."

Her eyes grew even wider. It had to be a human way to show excitement.

"What kind of probing would you prefer?" I

asked pleasantly. "In our lectures, they've taught us various methods but since it's the first time for both of us, I thought you should choose."

"What kinds are there?"

I grinned, satisfied that she was interested. "It all starts with the basic exam. Taking blood, measuring your body weight and size, counting your teeth, cutting off some of your mane for analysis, and so on. I have to admit that I've already completed most of that while I tended to your injuries. It was essential to be able to give you the best treatment possible, but I apologise. We can redo those things if you'd like."

Her lips parted but she didn't reply, so I continued. "The basic examination is usually followed by the actual probing. I can insert probes into your various orifices to look at your insides. I've read humans quite like anal probing, but as I said, it's your choice. I've prepared several different instruments to make it as pleasant for you as possible. What do you think about anal probing?"

The female coughed. I frowned, immediately worried that I'd overlooked an injury, but a quick look at my med scanner showed me that her lungs were intact. Maybe it was because we still hadn't given her that magical water humans required.

I rushed to the fabricator. I'd already programmed the chemical formula for water, so it took only seconds for a glass of liquid to appear in front of me. I offered it to the female and she grabbed it, downing it in one go.

"That wasn't poison, was it?" she asked as soon as she'd set down the glass. "Although, I guess that would be better than probing."

"No poisons, but I'm sure I could find some hallucinogens for you," I offered. "Or maybe some sedatives to make the probing even more comfortable."

"You mentioned lectures," she muttered. "What do you mean?"

"We're taking a course in alien abduction," Xil explained before I could. "We wanted to make sure that this abduction goes as smoothly as possible for everyone involved."

He didn't mention our previous failures.

"This is real? I'm really in an alien spaceship?"

Finally. I nodded. "Yes, you are. Should we repeat our introductory talk?"

"No, it's fine." She gulped visibly and I couldn't resist checking the med scanners once again to make sure her throat was alright. Maybe she'd had too much of that oxygen-hydrogen liquid. I'd have to do some more research into how much of it was safe for humans.

"Now that we've established this is real, could we progress to the probing?" Matar asked impatiently. "I've been looking forward to this too."

The female shook her head. "No probing."

"But it's part of the process," Xil argued. "There's no way around it. We may fail our assignment if we don't do it."

She made a strange noise that was somewhere between a cough and a laugh. "You're getting graded on this?"

"We are," I confirmed. "But don't worry, we've had excellent grades in the modules leading up to this. We're top of the class."

"Thank goodness for that."

Her voice had a strange vibration to it, but I hadn't read about this happening so I didn't know what that might mean. Excitement? Relief? There was so much learning to do. I was starting to think that humans were far more multi-faceted than I'd realised.

"Probing," Matar reminded us. "Now."

I walked over to my probing trolley that had all the instruments I'd require. I'd crafted most of them myself after studying human physiology. Most of the tools I'd have used for Kardarians were too big for our dainty little female. She was even smaller than I'd anticipated.

I chose one of the smallest tools and held it up so our female could see how unthreatening it looked. "Shall we start with the anal probing? Please roll around so I have better access. You can hand that sheet to Matar; I think subjects generally prefer being naked during probing."

She looked down at herself and grabbed the edge of the sheet covering her. "I'm naked," she stated.

"Yes, you are. I had to undress you when I looked after your injuries. Is that a problem? Did you want to experience the undressing while you're conscious?"

TRISH

This was one weird dream. I was starting to think that I was still lying by the side of the road, unconscious, having some strange concussion-induced visions. That was the only explanation. Even if I really had been abducted by aliens, I very much doubted that they'd ask my opinions about probing. Aliens didn't do that. They just did what they wanted before dropping you off back on Earth with your memory wiped. Or they sold you as slaves. Or...well, anything except this.

The blue alien seemed intent on stuffing that metal rod into my arse. I'd always loved anal sex - when I say always, I mean the two times my ex tried that with me before we split up - but this was something else entirely. What would happen if I said no? Would they still continue? They didn't seem intent on harming me, but they'd been brainwashed into thinking that this was part of the abduction process.

I laughed hysterically, causing them to look at me with confusion. Abduction process. Their words, not mine. Definitely a crazy dream.

"I'm glad you're happy about this," the blue alien - Havel, I believed - said with a grin. His fangs glistened in the bright light of the room, making a shudder run down my back. Maybe it was a good idea to do what they said. Those fangs looked lethal. I bet they were poisonous.

All three aliens were massive, hulking males full of hard muscles and tempting abs. They were drop-dead gorgeous, even with their scales, fangs, and tails. One tail. I couldn't help but look at it again. The green alien had rolled up his sleeves, exposing dark markings along his arms. Tattoos or birthmarks? Who knew. His tail was wrapped around his left leg like a snake, but I'd seen him pound the floor with it earlier. I wanted him to turn around so I could see if he had a hole in his (very tight) trousers where the tail sprouted from...his tail bone? Was it part of his bum? Or higher? I didn't dare ask him. He gave me the most dangerous vibes of the three of them. The yellow alien was the captain of the ship, but he had a good-natured smile on his face while he waited for the probing to begin. He'd shown me his mottled, scaled skin earlier. His shirt was still open, exposing pecs that were to die for.

My mouth watered at the sight. I shouldn't ogle them like that. They'd abducted me and were planning to stuff instruments into my - what had he called it? - orifices. My arse was just the beginning, I was sure of it. Another shiver ran down my back, but I wasn't sure if it was fear or excitement. It had been a while since I'd had anyone look at me with such fascination, even adoration.

Don't give in to the aliens, Trish. They've probably given you some drugs to make you fancy them. Maybe they played with my vision, too. What were the chances of all three of them looking this hot? Perhaps they were ugly monsters with tentacles and warts, and I only saw what I wanted to see.

"Are you speaking English?" I asked, suddenly realising how effortless our communication had been.

The yellow alien laughed. "No, we don't speak your primitive language. Havel fitted you with a translator as soon as we got you onto our ship. It's a brain slug, embedded in your right ear."

I must have misheard. Brain slug. He meant brain plug or something like that. Not slug. Not a slimy animal.

"They feed off soundwaves and then transmit the information right into your brain. You're speaking your language, but our slugs transform it into Kardarian. They've been fitted with microchips that can add whatever language we want. Because we weren't sure where on Earth we'd find you, we added all eight thousand languages spoken on Peritus."

I ignored every single thing he'd said and deleted

it from my memory. I was good at that. I'd experienced too much crap to want to remember it all.

Instead, I clung to the last word, one I hadn't heard before. "Peritus?"

"The intergalactic name for your planet. I'm not sure why you call it Earth. You've got so many oceans yet you didn't call it Sea or Ocean."

I cocked my head, surprised. I'd never thought of it like that.

"I have no idea why," I admitted. "Maybe it's because we all live on land. We're not made to live in the sea."

"Yes, you don't have any gills," the blue alien said with an almost disappointed look in his large, expressive eyes.

"Let's start the probing. Anal first?"

I couldn't believe this was happening. I was surrounded by aliens who wanted to look into my arse. With metal probes. And yet...my nipples were getting hard and warmth gathered between my legs. The thought turned me on. I was one crazy lady. I hadn't been with anyone in way too long; it was no surprise I was reacting like that. I was having sex withdrawal symptoms, that had to be it. That's why my mind was conjuring these things. Unless they were real.

That possibility was becoming more and more likely. I doubt even my mind could come up with brain slugs, especially not slugs embedded with microchips. That was one step too far.

"Turn around," the green alien ordered impatiently. "I'm starting to get hungry." His tail thumped on the floor as if to underline his words.

Time to make a decision...

"Is it going to hurt?" I asked, barely able to believe that I was actually considering it.

"Of course not," Havel replied with a frown as if that thought insulted him. "Unless you want it to. Is that what humans imagine alien probing to be like?"

I quickly shook my head. I didn't want to give him any ideas.

He seemed relieved at me not wanting it to hurt. And that relief was what made me turn onto my stomach. The white sheet slipped away, exposing my naked back. And my bum.

Had I shaved before I'd been abducted? It had been a couple of days, at least. Without a boyfriend, I often couldn't be bothered.

I snickered to myself. I was worried that the aliens might dislike a few hairs rather than fearing their probing.

"I've coated in the instrument in a cooling gel," Havel explained. "It will prevent pain and will help the probe glide in more easily."

Alien lube. How lovely. They'd really thought of everything. I wondered if that was part of their course. Had he practised this? Maybe on the other guys? The thought made me wet. Those three aliens, naked, probing each other...

Something cool touched my arse and all other thoughts fled my mind. Warm, soft hands spread my cheeks and the cold instrument was gently pressed against my rosebud.

I tensed, but then hands gently ran over my back and my shoulders and I instantly relaxed. I barely noticed the probe gliding into my arse, I was too occupied with one of the aliens massaging my shoulders. I didn't know if learning how to do this had been part of their strange abduction class, but if it had, I wanted to hug their teacher. It was heavenly.

"What now?" Havel whispered after he'd fully inserted the probe.

"What do you mean?" the captain asked. "Continue probing her."

"But this is it. I've inserted the probe. It's done. But it doesn't feel like it's enough."

"Wasn't there supposed to be a camera attached? To see her insides?"

The medic sucked in a breath. "I forgot! Klat, I'm an awful prober!"

He sounded genuinely upset, so much so that I turned my head to look at him.

"You're doing great. It feels lovely."

It really did. I was dripping wet even though none of them had touched me anywhere besides my back and my arse. The probe was slowly becoming warm while it filled me with a pleasant pressure. I ached to touch my clit, but that would have been entirely inappropriate. The aliens didn't seem to see this as something sexual. It was only me who was craving more.

"It does?" he asked, still unsure. "Shall I try another probe, a larger one?"

I straightened my neck again so they couldn't see my expression and grinned. "Yes, I think you should."

He pulled out the instrument, making me feel very empty indeed. I needed something bigger. An alien cock would have been perfect, but I'd settle for a larger probe.

I was crazy. I was being probed by aliens and I was *enjoying* it.

"Spread her open," Havel ordered, his voice hoarse. Maybe it wasn't just academic for him either.

Hands grabbed my cheeks and pulled them open. Cool air hit my opening just before cold metal was pressed against it once more. I tried to relax, but this one was a lot bigger than the one before. Havel pushed it in slowly, but with steady pressure, helping overcome my body's resistance. I moaned when it was fully inserted, stretching me. My clit was throbbing, aching to be touched.

"What a curious sound," the green alien muttered. I kept forgetting his name, but this wasn't the time to ask.

They kept stroking my back, my bum, even my

legs. My body was putty under their skilled hands as they massaged me into blissful oblivion. The probe in my arse seemed to get smaller, or maybe I was just getting used to the sensation of being filled to the brink. By now, I wouldn't have said no to an alien cock to complete the probing.

"Probe me," I moaned before realising I'd even done it.

Havel chuckled. "She seems to enjoy this. I think we'll get top grades on this."

"All credit goes to you, my friend," the captain replied before running his fingers through my hair. Now that he'd spoken, I could identify who of the guys were standing where and doing what to my body.

"Where shall we probe her next?" Matar asked.

"Female, do you want to continue?" Havel addressed me. "You still haven't told us your name."

"Trish," I groaned. "Don't stop."

The medic moved the probe in my arse and I almost came. Fuck. I was being probed by aliens and I was about to orgasm because of it. What was I turning into? Some sex hungry hussy ready to serve her alien masters? No way.

"We won't stop until you want us to, don't worry. Trish." He rolled the R in my name. I loved it. "Trish."

"Trish," the other two aliens echoed.

"I like that," Xil said, a smile audible in his voice. "We won't have to give you a new name."

I shouldn't be surprised that they were considering that as an option. These guys were crazy. And amazing at giving me pleasure.

"I'm going to remove the anal probe," Havel announced. "Then you're going to turn around so we can probe your other orifices."

That word took away some of my arousal. There had to be a better, sexier term for my holes.

"Don't," I moaned. "Keep it in. Do both at the same time."

Silence met my words. They hadn't expected that. I chuckled. It probably wasn't in their abduction course. Did that make it an extracurricular activity?

"Alright," the medic said after a while. "But turn to your side, we don't want you to get hurt. It'll be more comfortable that way."

The way he cared about my wellbeing while probing me was almost endearing. I was starting to think that these aliens had their hearts in the right place, despite their abduction fetish. They could have gone about it in a more violent manner, yet here they were, asking me how I wanted my probing to be done. Maybe that was why I wasn't reacting like a normal abduction victim should. Instead of running, screaming, attacking them, I was dripping wet and begging for a probe in my pussy.

I rolled onto my left and spread my legs. Matar grabbed my right leg and held it in position, saving me from having to expend any energy on it. I was now on full display, yet I didn't care.

"She's leaking," the captain said, sounding worried. "Female...Trish, is that normal? Are you unwell?"

"Normal," I managed to say before breaking into laughter. "Totally normal. Don't your females get wet when they're aroused?"

All three guys sucked in a breath, clearly shocked.

"No, they don't," Havel said after a moment's silence. "Is this water? Can I test it?"

For a moment, I thought he'd asked to taste it before I realised that he was a medic and probably interested in me from a scientific point of view.

"Go ahead," I offered, still laughing. "If your females don't have natural lubricants, doesn't it hurt them when you...you know. Wait, do you even have cocks? Like humans?"

This time, it was their turn to laugh.

"We do, sweet female," Matar chuckled. "Some of us even have more than just one."

I sat up a little to look at them. "What? More than one? How?"

Matar turned to the captain with an evil grin. "I think you'll have to show her, Xil."

"I don't think this is part of the probing," the yellow alien protested, his cheeks turning a dark ochre. "We're probing her, not she us."

"How many do you have?" I asked when he didn't start pulling down his trousers.

"Two," he replied without looking at me. "Some of us Kardarians are born with up to three. These two are lucky to only have one."

I frowned. "Why lucky? Most human men would happily have two dicks."

"It can get difficult. Even painful."

He didn't expand on that, leaving me burning with questions.

"If he gets an erection, he needs to get relief for both cocks," Havel explained, playing the helpful medic. "Most females don't like being penetrated by both at once and aren't always willing to be fucked twice, so he'll have to do it manually."

There were worse things. But also, what woman would say no to two alien cocks? I hadn't seen them yet, but the exoticness of it alone made me even wetter.

"To answer your other question," Havel continued, "we secrete a gel which gives us smoother access."

A gel. How neat. I wanted to see, feel, taste that.

"Let's proceed with the probing," Matar growled impatiently. "Black Oboto help me, it's getting uncomfortable watching her like that."

I shot him a look. His tail was no longer wrapped around his lower leg but had moved up instead, now protectively curled in front of his crotch, as if he didn't want me to see his erection. I wondered what that tail could do...

Something cool touched my nether lips and I gasped. I hadn't realised Havel had approached me with the second probe.

"Let me know if this is uncomfortable," he said softly and began to push in the probe. It felt like a smooth, metal dildo that was just the right size to stretch me without becoming painful. I moaned as my pussy sucked it in. Havel pushed in as far as he could before gently turning the probe, pushing it against my inner walls. I moaned loudly when the two probes touched, only separated by a thin layer of skin.

"Fuck," I groaned, barely clinging on to control.

"Does she want intercourse?" Xil asked.

All I could do was moan. Havel kept moving both probes, twisting and turning, making me quiver on the bed.

"I'm not sure," Havel replied. "I don't think it's part of the usual probing procedure. Maybe it's a human thing?"

"I need to go," the captain bit out and ran out of the room.

"He'll have his hands busy for a while," Matar teased, but I didn't care. I was teetering at the edge, ready to take the jump if only someone touched my clit. It looked like I'd have to do it myself.

I reached down and rubbed my bud. It only took

a single flick and I exploded, coming hard and fast. I moaned, whimpered, groaned, tossed from side to side, making the probes inside of me move and prolong the orgasm I was riding.

I didn't know what the two aliens were thinking or doing. All I cared about was the heat rushing through my body, the trembling originating in my core, the waves I didn't want to miss.

It took me forever to come back from my high. When I finally opened my eyes - I hadn't even realised I'd closed them - I was alone with Havel. He was still holding both probes, but his hands were shaking slightly.

"Can I pull them out now?" he asked cautiously as if he expected me to grind down on them again.

I nodded, not quite able to form words yet. My insides were still shaking. This had to have been one of my best orgasms ever - and it had been in front of three aliens who'd just abducted me. Not exactly what I'd imagined when I visualised having the most amazing orgasm.

Havel carefully removed the vaginal probe - with a squelching sound that made me blush - before slowly pulling out the anal probe. I felt empty and strangely alone as if I'd been abandoned.

Abandoned by alien probes. Now there was a blockbuster title.

LESSON 7

SEDUCTION FOR INEXPERIENCED MALES

MATAR

Xil found me in the engine room where I'd hidden after putting on a new uniform. I'd not had an accident like that since my metamorphosis when I'd first discovered the pleasures that previously boring body part could bring me.

"She's quite something," the captain stated.

I didn't turn around from the pipe I was hammering into submission. This blunt, physical work was just what I needed right now.

"Havel is cleaning her up, then he'll ask her about her probing experience so that we can submit her statement along with our assignment. I think she enjoyed it, so I'm expecting top marks for us."

I didn't care about grades. What I did care about was that my cock was already getting hard at the thought of Havel cleaning her between her legs. For our medic, this may have been strictly academic, but not for me. Nor for Xil.

"What have we done," I sighed. "I'm never going to be able to concentrate on my work again, not when I know she's on this ship. Did you see how she quivered? How hard her nipples were? How soft her skin felt?"

"Stop it or I'll have to take another cold shower," the captain growled. "But it's good to know we made the right choice when abducting her. She's perfect, more than perfect. She's a dream come true."

I nodded. "She really is. What's the next step now that she's been probed?"

"Seduction," he said, suddenly sounding a little worried. "We've never tried that before in our previous abduction attempts. Maybe that's why we always failed."

"It can't be that difficult, right? She was aroused by some simple probing, so we'll just offer to probe her again and she'll be happy. If we do it often enough, she'll get used to our touch and she might be willing to fuck without probes involved."

Xil laughed. "I don't think you understood the concept of seduction. It's not all about sex."

"It isn't?"

"No. I read this one paper on human courtship and it mentioned giving her plants. Not sure why, maybe because females like to eat healthy stuff?"

"We don't have any plants," I pointed out. "The fabricator can make vegetables, but I doubt it can make anything that's still alive and growing."

"Then we'll have to buy her one at the next space station we stop at. We should watch the next lecture as soon as possible so we know how to proceed. So far, everything Professor Katila has taught us has been effective."

He was right. I'd been worried this course might be a waste of time, but it had turned out to be the best thing we could have done. Thanks to the IGU, we now had our own female on board.

Our comms beeped simultaneously. Havel was paging us. I opened the call and his hologram appeared above my wrist, grinning at us.

"She's fallen asleep. I'm monitoring her vitals and will be alerted as soon as she wakes up, so how about we use the time to listen to the next lecture?"

Xil and I exchanged a look and grinned.

"We were just talking about that," I replied. "Meet you on the bridge?"

I gave the broken engine part one last longing look, then adjusted my uniform and followed Xil to the other end of the ship. I was never going to get any work done with our female around. She was sleeping and still I wasn't able to fix what needed fixing. This was going to be harder than I'd anticipated.

Havel was already on the bridge and had opened the lecture on the main viewscreen. I took my seat, crossed my arms in front of my chest - I didn't want to appear too eager - and waited for the Professor to speak.

"Hello, students. This lecture is split into two parts, depending on the purpose of your abduction. If you want your abductee for companionship and mating, continue watching. If you abducted her for other reasons like research or servitude, please skip to the second part now."

We waited in silence until she finally continued.

"This lecture may be called 'seduction for inexperienced males', but please be assured that this will be interesting for all genders and levels of experience. I like to say that learning is never over, no matter how good you think you are at a subject. I myself still like to expand my knowledge, even though I've conducted hundreds of successful abductions.

"Seduction isn't just about getting your abductee into your bed, nest, roost or whatever sleeping arrangement your species prefers. It's about forming a lasting bond that combines friendship with something deeper. Your end goal is to make your abductee love you with all her heart or hearts - or whatever anatomy her kind associate with love. You do not necessarily have to have the same feelings for your abductee, but it helps if you want to keep her as a long-term mate.

"Every species has different courtship rituals and it's your responsibility to research how your abductee likes to be wooed. You can combine that with the traditions of your own species, but make sure that at least half of your actions correspond to what your new female is used to. You don't want to confuse her unnecessarily.

"I know you will be eager to proceed as fast as possible, but be aware that seduction can take time. Start slowly, take note of how your female responds to your advances, then adjust your strategy accordingly. Give her your full attention. Make her feel adored and cherished. Protect her from all outside threats, even if you don't perceive them as important. Always remember that your abductee may never have left her planet before and everything is new and strange to her. A simple wormhole jump could traumatise her if you've not prepared her well.

"As your first assignment in this module, I'd like you to make a list of all the seduction strategies you've read about during the research phase. Then sort them by intensity. If you have the choice between giving her a sweet treat versus marking her with your saliva, choose the former to start with. If you find a strategy that works well for your abductee, repeat it again and again, even if it becomes boring to you. Your abductee will let you know when she's ready to proceed to the next step."

She smiled, her third eye glazed over as if she was reminiscing over a past abduction. I was impressed that she'd abducted hundreds of beings. I hadn't thought it possible for a Karangi, known for their benevolence and kindness, to do this kind of work professionally, but maybe Professor Katila was an exception to her species' customs.

"Before we end this lecture, please be reminded to submit your practical assignment reports as soon as possible. Seduction is not part of the abduction assignment so you don't need to wait to complete this module before submitting your reports. However, if your probing went exceptionally well, you may include a short summary of it in your assignment."

Havel grinned happily at that. I was sure he expected us to get bonus points for our successful probing.

Xil switched off the screen, also smiling. This crew had never been happier. Even my own lips curved into a smile. I wasn't used to that movement. I was known for being grumpy and I did my best to live up to that expectation.

"Havel, finish your report," Xil commanded. "I'll read over it when you're done, but I think you're best placed to write it. Definitely mention the probing and if our female agrees, include a quote from her. Maybe have her rate the probing on a scale from one to ten."

"I'll be disappointed if she says anything lower than nine," Havel muttered. "Although, I did forget the cameras so..."

"Matar and I will make a list of seduction strategies," the captain interrupted. "Hopefully, we'll be done with that before she wakes up so that we can get started right away. I want her to be ready for mating as soon as possible."

His eyes flicked down to his crotch and I couldn't help but follow his gaze. He was hard, just like me. Havel was already walking out of the room so I couldn't see if he had an erection too, but I wouldn't have been surprised if he had. This female was messing with our bodies already and she hadn't even touched us.

With a sigh, I created a piece of virtual paper and began jotting down what I'd read during the Learn phase of the 4 Ls. I felt Xil watching me, but I didn't pay him any attention. I was intent on doing well with this seduction thing and hopefully be the first our female decided to mate with.

1. Opening doors for her (*note to self: programme doors not to open automatically*)
2. Give her a plant (*note to self: research what colours she likes*)
3. Sing to her while she's a floor above from you (*does it work if she's in the same room?*)
4. Write love letters (*are comms acceptable or do we have to procure real paper?*)
5. Sit next to her while someone else plays a string instrument (*may be difficult to find a musician; research if recorded music or a live stream of a musician is acceptable*)
6. Have food together and have a fire burning instead of normal lights
7. Give her lots of boxes full of tiny food pieces
8. Wear lacy undergarments

9. Write poetry (*note to self: find a poetry generator*)
10. Send yourself (*not sure what is meant by this, more research needed*)
11. Watch recordings of other couples
12. Smile a lot and swirl your moustache (*should we get fake facial hair?*)
13. Hold her hand as often as possible

Xil looked over my shoulder.

"That's a great list," he muttered. "You really did your research."

It made me feel surprisingly good to hear that from him. It wasn't that I didn't feel appreciated on this ship, but this was something unfamiliar and I had never expected to be good at it.

"I don't quite get the bit about lacy undergarments," Xil said thoughtfully. "What does lacy mean?"

"Fabric full of holes," I supplied, glad I'd looked that up a few days ago. "It should be easy to replicate."

"I don't wear undergarments. Do you think it's essential?"

"It came up again and again," I sighed. "I'm not happy about it either, but humans seem to see this as an essential seduction strategy. They call it lingerie, I believe. We could even cut up some of our uniform trousers. I don't think it matters as long as there are lots of holes."

"Enough holes for our dicks to be seen?"

"Exactly. I think it's supposed to be a teasing thing, where she can see our assets but would still have to undress us."

Xil licked his lips. "That does sound tempting, now that you say it like that. But that's probably for later, we should start with something where we're fully clothed. I wouldn't want to overwhelm her." He tapped on his comms, then looked at me triumphantly. "I've locked her door, so now she can't exit her room without one of us opening the door for her. That should be a great start to our seduction."

I nodded. "Great thinking. Let's put the door opening in first place. I suppose she might be hungry when she wakes up, so we can give her tiny food pieces next. For some reason, humans eat them out of a box rather than from a plate, but the fabricator should be able to replicate that. What next?"

"We'll have to wait until we arrive at the space station before we can get her a flower or a string instrument. I won't allow open fire on this ship so we can't do that until we're back on Kardar. We could write her letters though, maybe even now while she's asleep, and then she can read them when she wakes. I bet Havel could even come up with some poetry."

Xil raised his eyebrows. "Havel? Poetry? You're kidding."

"If not, we can probably find a way to generate some simple poetry. Or we'll look in a human book for something some human male has written in the past. I doubt she'll know every human book by heart, so she'll never notice. Especially if we use a really old book."

"Good idea. We can also do the singing from a floor below, but we have to plan that so that one of us is with her to see her reaction. Maybe two of us can sing so it's loud enough to penetrate the walls."

I rubbed my tail, a clear sign that I was getting nervous. "Why do you think we have to sing in another room? Do humans not like it when they see someone else sing? Does it destroy the attraction?"

"You were the one who put it on the list, I'd never heard of it," Xil admitted. "I could sing a drinking song, or maybe a lullaby my mother-"

"Drinking song," I interrupted. We didn't want her to go to sleep. We wanted to mate with her and it was essential that she was awake during that. I wanted to hear her make those sweet sounds again, where she sounded like she was in a happy sort of pain. Pleasant distress.

"Havel can join you," I said. "I'll be with her since it was my idea."

Xil didn't look happy about it but then inclined his head. "Then I shall deal with the tiny food pieces. She's small, so I suppose they have to be even tinier than they'd be for us. Size of my fingernails, maybe?"

I nodded. "That or smaller. She really is tiny."

"What kind of food should I get? Maybe something from Kardar to introduce her to our cuisine?"

"Make a mixture of Kardarian and Peritan food," I suggested. "That way we'll see what she likes best."

I quickly sorted the list anew and added some notes for Havel, since he hadn't been here with us.

1. Opening doors for her (*Havel, we've locked her door*)
2. Give her lots of boxes full of tiny food pieces (*Xil will do this*)
3. Write love letters and poetry
4. Xil and Havel will sing drinking songs while Matar is with her a floor above
5. Wear lacy undergarments
6. Watch recordings of other couples
7. Hold hands whenever possible

<u>In future:</u>

1. Give her a plant (*note to self: research what colours she likes*)
2. Sit next to her while someone else plays a string instrument (*may be difficult to find a musician; research if recorded music or a live stream of a musician is acceptable*)

3. Have food together and have a fire burning instead of normal lights

I deleted the bit about facial hair and sending ourselves since I didn't know how that would contribute to seducing Trish. Maybe if all our other strategies didn't work, we could return to that.

"We can get Havel to find recordings of human couples," I suggested when I was done with the list. "I'm sure he came across some when he was researching human psychology and physiology."

"Yes, he showed me some," Xil said with a wide grin. "Humans can be very flexible when they want to be."

TRISH

As soon as I woke, the memories of what happened made me sit up straight. I wasn't confused at all. I knew exactly what happened. It made me both queasy and breathless. A sexy kind of breathless, that is. I'd been probed by aliens. For real. And I'd enjoyed it. It was so amazing that I passed out in the end after the best orgasm of my life. I dimly remembered one of them carrying me into a sort of shower and washing me, but I had no recollection of him bringing me into this bedroom.

It was tiny, reminding me of a ship's cabin. I guessed that's what it was, now that I thought about it. The bed was attached to the wall and looked like it could be pulled up, creating more space. Metal shelves and cupboards graced the walls to create as much storage as possible. Instead of a window, a large screen hung opposite the door. It was blank though. No alien soaps for me to watch.

They'd dressed me in a simple dress that resembled a pale blue sack with holes for my head and arms. Not exactly the height of fashion, but I supposed I should be grateful I wasn't still naked. They'd even provided a pair of slippers made from something that reminded me of felt, yet it was softer beneath my feet.

My stomach growled, reminding me that it had been a while since my last meal. How long had I been on this ship? I knew neither how long I'd been unconscious when they'd abducted me nor how long I'd just slept. For all I knew, I could have been here for days. A shiver ran down my back at the thought. Would anyone miss me? Chadra would probably be the only one, mostly because I destroyed her scooter and couldn't pay for the damage. She might also miss having me for small jobs that she didn't want to do herself.

I got up. It was time to explore this spaceship, hopefully without stumbling upon one of the aliens. I needed some time to process what had happened.

Problem was, the door didn't have a knob or handle. I stepped close to it, hoping it might have a sensor that would open it automatically, but nothing happened. I pressed my hands against it and pushed, without success.

They'd locked me in like a prisoner. I supposed it was to be expected. They'd abducted and probed me. For some reason, they were intent on following every alien abduction stereotype imaginable, which I guessed included being locked into a room. At least this wasn't a cell. And I had clothes. I should be grateful for small mercies like that.

I banged my fists against the door and started shouting for them to open it. Just like I was supposed to behave, right? I couldn't help but laugh at the absurdity of the situation. I hadn't just been abducted by aliens. I was part of some kind of academic assignment they were conducting and therefore had to be the perfect abduction victim. This was ridiculous.

"Let me out!" I yelled as loud as I could.

I looked around the room again, almost hoping to spot a camera that I could wave to. Or destroy. Both options sounded tempting.

"Aliens, come and unlock this door!"

Footsteps sounded in the distance. Someone was running towards me. Had they heard my calls or was this just a coincidence? Maybe their cameras were too hidden for me to see. It didn't make sense for there not to be any. I had been abducted; of course, they'd want to keep an eye on me and see if the probing had any aftereffects. I bet the blue medic, Havel, would be keen to document everything I did. It was almost endearing if I hadn't been kidnapped.

The door slid open, revealing a grinning Matar. The green, tailed alien seemed pleased at himself for some reason, even though I scowled at him.

"Why did you lock me up?" I snapped. It was probably a bad idea to snap at my captors, but I was hungry and to be honest, after the probing I didn't take them too seriously. I didn't think they were dangerous, but there was a high chance I was wrong. Perhaps this was my mind trying to protect me from the truth.

"So I could open the door for you," he replied as if that made any sense at all. "Are you pleased?"

"No. I'm not."

His face fell, disappointment distorting his alien features. It was strange how his expressions were so human, in a way, or at least similar enough for me to recognise his emotions.

"Do you not like doors being opened for you?" he asked, sounding a little unsure.

"I don't like locked doors," I shot back at him. "Am I your prisoner?"

He raised his eyebrows and I noticed how perfectly shaped they were. Just like everything about him. He was gorgeous from top to bottom, even his tail. Alright, maybe his tail wasn't gorgeous, but it was exotic and strangely attractive. It made me want to reach out and see if it would curl around my hand.

"You're not. You're going to be our mate."

He - or one of the others - had said that before. A joke, surely? I wasn't mate material. I wasn't their species, nor was I particularly beautiful. Only pretty girls got abducted, that was universally acknowledged. Or maybe clever ones, to work for them and tell them all of Earth's secret. I was neither.

"I'm not. I want you to return me to my home." I stood as straight as I could and looked him right in the eyes. It took all my willpower to do that. His gaze was intense, sucking me in. His eyes were as green as the rest of him, but small silver specks shimmered within his pupils, making them sparkle. They had to be the most beautiful eyes I'd ever seen.

I forced myself to look away. I didn't want to swoon over my abductor. This wasn't the time to develop Stockholm syndrome.

"That isn't possible," he said surprisingly gently. "We'd fail our assignment. But don't worry, we'll look after you. We've already made a list-"

He broke off and bit his lower lip as if he'd said more than he'd intended.

"A list?"

"Of things to make you happy," he admitted. "Opening doors is on there, but it seems you don't like that. I shall erase it immediately."

A white rectangle appeared in front of him, covered in small, neat writing. I tried to read it, but it was written in *alien*. Whatever language they spoke. The translator - I didn't call it the disgusting thing it really was - only worked for spoken words, it seemed. And I was fine with that. I didn't want a worm in my eyes, thank you very much.

Matar ran his fingers over the projection and the top line disappeared. On one hand, I was curious about what else lay in store, while on the other hand, I dreaded to find out. Being locked inside my room just so he could open a door for me wasn't a good start. What would be next, starving me so they could sate my hunger?

My stomach growled again. Matar jumped back, his tail erect, his eyes wild as he searched the corridor for a threat.

I rolled my eyes. "It's just my stomach. I'm hungry."

He frowned. "Your stomach speaks? Is that normal for humans?"

"It doesn't speak. It makes growly noises."

Matar shook his head. "No, it spoke. Loud and clear. It said 'electricity'. Or maybe 'power', those words are very similar in my language."

This time, it was me who stared at him in confusion. "I assure you, my stomach doesn't talk. It has no mind of its own. It was just a grumble."

The green male didn't look as if he believed me,

but he let it drop. "Xil is preparing food for you right now. Come, I'll take you to our canteen. I shall show you the ship afterwards, especially the floor above."

"What's there?" I asked curiously as I started following him.

"You'll see," he hedged.

We ignored several locked doors along the brightly lit corridor, heading straight to a large, open-plan room that seemed to act as both kitchen and living area. Most tables and chairs were covered with...things. Empty plates. Random gadgets. Electronics I didn't recognise. Something that looked like a yellow bath duck but definitely wasn't one. These guys didn't like to tidy up, that much was clear. I'd give them a minus point for that. When you invited someone into your home, you cleaned it first or at least made it look less like a mancave.

Matar seemed to realise the issue and simply wiped off all the contents from the closest table, beckoning me to sit on the only empty chair. I shrugged and took my seat, waiting for him to join me. He kept standing though, his tail knocking on the floor as if he was nervous. He pressed some buttons on the computer thingy he had on his wrist.

"She's here, klatting get to the canteen now," he snapped at whoever he was talking to.

"On my way."

That was the captain's voice if I wasn't mistaken.

"He's prepared food for you. I hope it'll be what you imagined."

I frowned at him. "I didn't imagine anything. It's not like I planned to be abducted. I guess I should be happy you're feeding me at all."

"Of course we're feeding you," he replied, clearly offended at the thought of letting me starve. "It's what good abductors do. We're going to look after you from now on. Whatever you want, just tell us and we'll make sure you get it."

"Really? Whatever I want?"

He grimaced. "Within reason. If you want a lavva fruit or a tribitt, that's doable. If you want a bigger spaceship or a weapon of mass destruction, it would be less likely that we can fulfil your wish."

"What's a tribitt? My translator didn't get that one."

"A furry, long-eared animal that many Kardarians keep as pets, especially females. They're fluffy and quite intelligent but also very mischievous. I'm not sure what our Captain would say about having a pet on the Jade though."

I grinned. "I want one."

Matar looked as if he regretted this conversation. "You need to ask Xil-"

"Ask me what?"

The captain had entered the canteen without me noticing. I whirled around and took in his broad, muscular form. During the probing, I'd been kind of out of it, but now I took the chance to look at him properly. His head was bald, just like that of the other two, but strange ochre patches made it look less bare. The same mottled jaguar pattern he had all over his body - I remembered when he'd torn open his shirt to show me. The skin on his face and scalp was smooth, like that of a human, no scales like on his chest. Of the three men, he was the most human-looking, if you ignored his bright yellow skin colour, his scales and his dark orange eyes that didn't have lashes.

His dark blue uniform had silver stripes along his arms and legs, only highlighting how his bulk stretched the fabric. Why did they have a uniform when this ship wasn't military? And they were only three guys living on the Jade, so it didn't make sense to me. Maybe some weird alien tradition, just like their desire to probe humans.

"She wants a tribitt," Matar sighed.

To my surprise, Xil shrugged. "Then we shall get one. We should reach Kepler Two in about a week, so until then, we can make a list of everything Trish needs." He gave me a warm smile and held out a metal box. "For you."

Was he giving me a present? These aliens were so weird. Half of the time I didn't know if they were serious or if this was just some kind of twisted game. Maybe they were toying with me, waiting until I felt safe only to pull the floor from under my feet and show me their true, monstrous natures. I mean, what kind of alien gave the woman he'd abducted a gift?

I sat it down on the table and carefully opened the lid, half expecting poisonous scorpions or other lethal critters ready to sting me. But no. Inside was a grid made of something that looked like shimmering plastic, separating the box into thirty-two compartments, each of them filled with some kind of food. At least I thought it was food.

The portions were tiny, the size of half of my thumb. Xil had taken finger food to a new level. Some of them didn't even constitute one bite. How small did he think my mouth was?

One compartment contained a single blue leaf. Was that even edible? Next to it was something that looked like a bright pink mealworm. No thanks. Some of the *things* were clearly meat, while others could have been meat, plant, or something in between. Nothing looked familiar at all. I supposed they hadn't used their stop on Earth to restock.

"Do you like it?" Xil asked. He was watching me intently, clearly eager to get a reaction out of me. It was almost adorable, having this big, dangerous alien begging for my approval.

"Is that how you eat?"

His enthusiasm turned into confusion. "No. We eat proper portions. Isn't this what human males give their females when they want to seduce them?"

Why would I want-

"Chocolates." I started laughing. "This is what a box of chocolates looks like. Now I get it."

"What's chocolates?" Matar asked. He looked just as downtrodden and disappointed as Xil. I felt sorry for them and tried to contain my laughter. It was hard though. This was hilarious.

"Chocolate is a sweet deliciousness made from cocoa beans. You can get it in all shapes and forms, but if you go on a date, the guy might give the woman a box of chocolates. Small, expensive ones with different fillings." I looked down at the box. They'd kind of got the concept...except that they'd used normal food instead of chocolate. I couldn't help but smile at Xil. "You did well, it's almost the same. Thank you."

A grin lit up his face and his cheeks turned a darker yellow. An alien blush, how very sweet. I was starting to realise that there was something sweet and cuddly inside those big, burly men.

"Try them," Matar encouraged me. "That red piece is grilled oro steak, a delicacy from our home planet."

It didn't look like it had been grilled or cooked in any way. It was bloody. Or maybe that was a sauce. I told myself it was red gravy and gingerly took the piece of meat. I gave it a cautious sniff, but it actually smelled quite nice, like peri-peri chicken.

I wasn't a picky person. If you were poor, you ate whatever you found, even if it was out of date, dirty or come from shady sources. This was alien food, however. There may be harmful substances in there. Germs my body wasn't used to.

"Havel has made sure it's all safe for you to eat," Matar reassured as if he could read my mind. Maybe he could. I didn't know anything about their species.

"Where is he?" I asked to stall for time. As appetising as the meat smelled, as disgusting did it look as it oozed with red fluid.

"Practicing," Xil replied, then pursed his lips. "Ignore I said that. It's a surprise."

That sounded ominous. A drop of liquid fell from the piece of meat, landing on a white disk that looked like a tiny pancake. It immediately turned a disgusting shade of orange.

"That's strange," Matar muttered. "Must be some kind of chemical reaction." He took the mini pancake and gave it a sniff. "Do you mind if I taste this, female?"

"My name is Trish. And go ahead."

He bit off a tiny piece, leaving teeth marks on the disk. His teeth were triangular. Weird. But not the weirdest thing I'd seen since waking up on this spaceship.

"Still tastes good. Those are some of my favourites."

He put the half-finished pancake back in its place in the box. Eating something someone else had bitten into didn't seem to be against their etiquette. A pancake with blood and alien spittle. Just what I'd always dreamed off. Still, it looked more appetising than the meat I was still holding.

I squeezed my eyes shut and almost threw the piece of meat into my mouth. It was chewy as if it had been cooked for too long, but it didn't taste bad. The spices were different from anything I'd ever eaten before, but definitely edible. This wouldn't become my favourite food though. The aftertaste was strangely sour, making me wish for something sweet. Maybe that pancake?

I took it, not hesitating this time.

I gagged as soon as its flavour registered. It tasted like puke. I spit it out, catching it in my hand. At least I hadn't thrown up all over the box. That should count for something.

"Not to your taste?" Xil chuckled, not seeming to be offended. "Try some of the plants. Havel said humans must eat a lot of plants. Something about mini vitas."

"Vitamins." I grinned. "What would you recommend?"

He pointed at a ball of cooked leaves that reminded me of spinach. It was even green. That seemed safe.

Still, it took some force of will to nibble on it. The nibble turned into happy chewing as flavours of cinnamon and caramel caressed my tongue. Now this was what I'd expect a suitor to give me. If all their vegetables tasted this good, I was going to become a vegetarian.

"Do you have more of that?" I asked as soon as I'd reluctantly swallowed that amazingness.

Xil nodded. "I can make you an entire bowl. But first, you need to go with Matar. Havel is ready." He pointed at his wrist computer as if that meant anything to me.

What were they going to do next? More probing? Likely, if Havel was involved. He was deeply passionate about it. He'd even asked me questions about how I'd found the probing while he'd cleaned me, but I couldn't quite remember what I'd answered. It was all a bit of a blur.

I left the weird food box on the table and followed Matar to a circular column at the other end of the room.

He pressed his hand against what looked like smooth bronze metal and it rotated until an opening appeared. The inside of the column was lit up with fluorescent blue lights.

Matar stepped inside and again put his hand on the wall before realising that I hadn't followed him.

"It's the elevator," he explained with a smirk. "It'll take us upstairs."

"It's very small."

His tail waggled. Like a happy dog's. "Yes. It is. We'll have to stand very close."

"Can't we go one after the other?"

"No, it's not programmed to your biosignature yet. The captain can do that later, but we don't have time. Come on. I won't hurt you."

Strangely enough, that hadn't been my worry. That scared me a little. I should have been afraid of him, of all three aliens, but I wasn't. I just didn't want to be pressed against him, feeling all those muscles...

Or maybe I did want to. But I shouldn't. It was a bad idea.

With a sigh, I stepped into the elevator, pointedly turning my back to Matar. I left a few inches between us, but sighed again when I realised the column doors couldn't close like that. I shuffled back, careful to avoid touching him, but he wrapped his arms around my waist and pulled me against his chest.

The doors slid close and with them, any chance of getting out of his embrace. His hands were tight on my hips, holding me in place. His chest was hard against me while something even harder pressed into my lower back. Heat shot into my core, making me just as aroused as he was. Fuck. This wasn't happening. I couldn't be horny.

I wriggled against him, but he didn't let go of me. No, he groaned, clearly pleased I'd rubbed his cock. Unintentionally. Totally unintentionally.

Luckily, the door opened again, revealing an unfamiliar corridor. I hadn't even felt the elevator moving, but to be honest, I had been a little distracted by Matar's erection. Did he have one or two cocks? I knew Xil had two but I couldn't remember if Matar had mentioned how many he had. I snorted. What a strange world in which a girl would have to find out how many dicks her partner had.

Matar reluctantly let me go and I jumped forward, putting several feet of space between us. It was safer that way.

"Come, this way." He pushed past me, not trying to touch me. I was both relieved and disappointed. I hurried after him until we got to two massive double doors, looking much thicker than any I'd seen before. Matar typed something into his wrist communicator and the doors slid open. A blast of warm, smelly air hit me at the same time as my ears were assaulted by the noise of a rocket launch. Well, not quite as loud, but it almost made me want to cover my ears.

"One moment, I thought he'd switched them off," Matar muttered and continued pressing buttons. I took the time to peek into the room. Lots of pipes, wires, lights, and cables surrounded six large columns similar to the one the elevator had been housed in. In the centre of the circular room was a glass ball filled with a flickering green flame. I had no idea what any of it was, but it didn't need a genius to figure out this was the engine room.

With a hiss, the noise stopped, leaving only blissful silence.

"Ten minutes," he announced. "Then I have to turn them on again."

I had no idea why he'd even turned them off. I hadn't asked him to show me the engines. I wasn't good with electronics even on Earth and I bet these machines were a lot more advanced than anything I'd find back home, even on the spaceport. I'd never been inside a human-made spaceship, but I doubted it was anything like this one.

Matar put a hand on the small of my back, gently pushing me into the room. I let him, revelling at how good his touch felt. I became aware of the heat between my legs once more. What was this alien doing to me?

When we got to the green flame, the metal floor gave way to a grate, revealing the room beneath us. And down there stood Havel and Xil, looking up with grins on their faces.

"What's going on?" I asked Matar, but he didn't reply. His hand was still on my back. I should've stepped back from him, but my legs didn't move.

Something nudged my leg. I looked down only to find his tail possessively curling around my knee.

"Your tail is touching me," I whispered.

"So it is."

"Why is it doing that?"

"Sometimes it's hard to control it. Many, many generations ago, all Kardarians had tails. They were like an extra limb and we could use them as such.

Now, only some of us are still born with tails and those who do have lost the ability to fully control their tails. With some practice, it's possible to get rudimentary control, but when I don't concentrate on it, it sometimes takes on a life of its own."

A sentient tail? I had a hard time believing that. Maybe he simply wanted an excuse to touch me.

I didn't get a chance to interrogate him further. Beneath us, Xil and Havel opened their mouths and began to howl in unison. It sounded like they were in agony. Were they being attacked? Their howls turned louder and louder, tearing at my heartstrings.

"Help them!" I shouted at Matar, panic freezing my mind and body.

"You want me to join them?"

He didn't sound worried at all. Just confused.

"Do something!" I cried, unable to take their pained yowling much longer.

In an instant, his hands were on my hips again and he spun me around. Before I knew what was happening, his lips were on mine.

LESSON 8

THE MATING HABITS OF HUMANS

HAVEL

"It's working!" I shouted jubilantly, breaking the song.

Xil stopped too, looking up with a surprised expression. He hadn't expected our singing to be this effective either.

Above us, Matar and Trish were kissing. She was wrapped in his arms, her lips on his. My cock twitched with jealousy. It should have been me up there. I was the one who'd successfully probed her. It was me who'd introduced her to our abduction skills. I remembered how it had felt to slide the probe inside her, imagining that it was my cock...

"I can't believe that worked," Xil muttered. "I would have bet against it. Why did our singing make her kiss him? Shouldn't she come running to kiss us?"

We watched as their kiss turned more and more passionate. Xil's jealousy was almost palpable, or maybe I was projecting my own onto him.

"Let's go," I growled after a few minutes. "At least this might mean that she'll be ready for the next stage."

Xil's frown lessened. "Mating."

"Kissing is a good step towards that. I was worried humans might not be into kissing, but it looks like they love it as much as Kardarians. Let's hope they love to fuck even more."

The probing had shown that she was compatible with us. She would need some time to adjust, but she'd be able to take us. Maybe even Xil's two cocks at once. Luckily, they were one above the other and not next to each other like with some other alien species. That would have made finding a position awkward, but like this, he could rut her from behind in true Kardarian fashion.

"Have you prepared a room?" I asked as we left Matar and Trish alone.

"Yes, I did that after I made her food. She didn't like most of it, by the way. We'll need to experiment some more."

"That was to be expected. Her palate will be used to some vastly different things. It's a pity we couldn't find more human recipes for our replicator."

He shrugged. "She'll just have to get used to it. But yes, the room is ready. I had the bots build a bed large enough for all of us. I also prepared some underclothes with holes in. Now you just have to select some videos of human couples to watch. I don't know if Kardarian couples work, so let's not risk it."

I nodded. "I've got some videos I found during the early research phase when we started to consider humans. I'm sure one of them will work."

I didn't mention that I'd watched them many, many times, and not for strictly academic reasons. Watching humans fuck was hot. I understood why human couples might watch that together, although I didn't understand why they ate plant seeds while doing so. I wanted to kiss her and then maybe replicate some of the positions, not eat. Well, maybe eat her... I'd tried some of the juices that had leaked out of her. The taste had almost made me come by itself. I ached to taste her once again.

No plant seeds for her. Definitely not. There were going to be no distractions that could stand in the way of our mating.

I followed Xil into the room he'd prepared. It was one of the storage rooms, but he'd managed to turn it into a cosy space by adding soft lights and fabrics. I'd never taken him for an interior designer, but I had to admit he'd done a stellar job, especially in the short time he'd had.

My comms beeped and as soon as I saw who the message was from, I activated the holo screen so that Xil could see it too.

"Professor Katila's marked our assignment already," I told him, my voice shaking a tiny bit. I wanted to do well, but had we done enough to pass?

"It's not the probing grade," I said after opening the attachment. "It's for the abduction itself."

"I don't want to look," Xil admitted. "Just tell me if we passed or not."

"Choosing on physiology alone lacked insight... needed assistance from teacher... good choice of abductee... initial speech overwhelming..."

"Tell me," Xil growled. "Now."

I quickly scrolled to the end and my hearts skipped a beat. "We passed. Just about. I can't believe she detracted points for calling her for help. She keeps telling us to ask questions so she shouldn't penalise us for it. And we didn't choose her just because of her boobs..."

Xil put a hand on my mouth, silencing me. "We passed. That's all that counts."

He looked happier than I'd ever seen him. "Does that mean we've passed the entire course?"

"Mmmmmrmmppfhh."

He removed his hand, allowing me to speak with an apologetic wink.

"No. All our grades will be added up and then an average will be calculated. This practical assignment is weighed pretty high though, so unless we did really badly in other parts of the course, we should pass."

Another bing interrupted me. Our probing grades had arrived.

My fangs extended as nerves threatened to take the better of me. I was desperate for a top grade in this. I'd thrown my hearts and soul into preparing for our female's probing and I thought it had gone exceptionally well. Professor Katila had counted the speech into the abduction assignment, so I didn't have to worry about that. It was only the probing and that had gone splendidly, right? We'd made our little abductee come. That alone should give us the highest grade possible.

"Do you want me to?" Xil offered when I didn't open the message.

I nodded, suddenly feeling weak in my knees. This was just a grade, just a test. But no, it was so much more. My honour as a medic was at stake. I had to do well. Had to.

"She praises your preparation and dedication... she likes that you created your own probes... but you shouldn't have offered our abductee a choice..."

"But that would have been impolite!" I protested. "I wanted her to feel safe and by giving her control over what was happening, she felt more confident."

Xil shrugged. "Just saying what Professor Katila wrote. Let me continue."

I sighed and sat down on the bed. I was starting to think we might not get a good a grade on this as I'd hoped.

"Us touching her was unprofessional," the captain grunted. "We should have restrained her instead. And she says your probing was useless. It held no scientific value because your probes didn't actually film her insides or measure things like her temperature."

I stared at him, unbelieving. "But..."

"We failed," Xil interrupted. "We klatting failed."

"It can't be. It went so well. She even said that she enjoyed the probing. I-"

I covered my face in my hands. The day had

started so well yet now, I just wanted to punch something. Or someone, namely Professor Katila.

"She says the abductee should not have been consulted on whether she liked the probing or not, at least not during the procedure," Xil said, still reading our results. "And while the Professor appreciates that we didn't want to harm her, the probing turned sexual rather than academic, especially with all of us touching her."

He grimaced. "I don't regret touching her boobs."

I didn't regret probing her either. It had been a special experience and I wouldn't let the Professor taint the memory of it. Of course, we hadn't wanted to hurt our female. She was going to be ours for the rest of our lives and starting that relationship with pain was a bad idea. Surely our teacher understood that?

Klat.

"We failed one and passed one," Xil summarised. "What's next?"

"They'll take a look at all the reports we've submitted since we started the course. If our average grade means we've failed, there'll be a final interview with both us and the abductee...Trish. That could save us."

The captain looked grave. "Let's assume that we failed the reports too. That means that Trish's opinion could mean life or death for us. In a figure of speech, anyway. I guess the course doesn't matter as much, not now that the abduction was successful."

"True, but I still want to pass."

"Me too," he admitted. "It would feel like a failure if we don't. We can't do much about our own interviews, but we can make sure Trish only has the best to say about us. We need to make the mating a success. We've prepared well, but will it be enough?"

"We've got a large bed, lacy underclothes and recordings of human couples. We can also hold hands while lying on the bed to tick off another seduction strategy. Plus Matar is kissing her just now, that should count for a lot."

I wished it was me in Matar's position. I couldn't wait to feel her lips against my fangs, my venom dripping onto her tongue. Our ancestors' venom could be lethal, but what we were left now only had a slightly intoxicating effect, increasing positive emotions and sensations. Fanged Kardarians were highly prized prostitutes for that reason.

"Let's get changed," Xil said and produced a stack of black clothes. Those had to be the ones he'd made. I wasn't keen on wearing something when in bed with Trish, but if it was their tradition to wear damaged clothes, then so be it. Maybe she'd take pleasure in making the holes even bigger so she could access my cock.

I changed in record time, eager to be ready in case Matar and Trish joined us. I ended up wearing a black shirt than only covered the top half of my chest - and that only in pieces since holes and loose threads were too copious to count - and tight black leggings with one leg longer than the other. Again, Xil had made sure to add as many holes as possible without tearing the fabric into pieces.

His own outfit was similar, except that he wore shorts that didn't leave a lot to the imagination. One of his balls was clearly visible, while his two cocks strained against the fabric. Maybe we should provide Trish with some scissors to make it easier to unwrap us.

Xil left Matar's clothes by the door. He'd just have to get changed as quickly as possible once he got here.

While the captain went to get some drinks, including the water liquid Trish needed for survival, I chose one of my favourite human copulation videos. It had two males and one female in it. Hopefully, that wasn't too removed from tradition. I could have chosen a couple, but I thought this would make it more obvious to our female that all three of us wanted to get involved with her. We'd abducted her together and we'd mate her together. Maybe not all at the same time since she lacked the orifices for that.

XIL

When I returned to the bedroom, I met Matar and Trish in the corridor just outside. Her lips were red and swollen. Had Matar hurt her? If so, I'd punch him until his green skin turned blue.

She stared at me as if she hadn't seen me before. Had he taken her mind while kissing? Anger roared through me and I barely managed to hold onto the tray topped with four drinks.

"What are you wearing?" she asked in a strange voice. Her eyes wandered up and down my body, lingering on my crotch for a long time. I checked to make sure neither of my cocks was showing, but they were mostly hidden, with only some of my skin peeking beneath the black fabric.

"Clothes, with holes," I said proudly. "Do you like it?"

"Holes..." she muttered, clearly impressed. Her face did weird things, contorting and quivering.

"Is everything alright?" I asked, starting to get concerned at her behaviour. Matar had to have damaged her.

When she didn't reply, I turned to him, growling. "What did you do to her?"

He flinched. "Nothing. We kissed. A lot." He smiled sheepishly. "And my tail may have slipped under her clothes."

I gaped at them. He'd started the mating process

without us? Had he penetrated her with his tail? This was completely out of order.

"Get inside, change," I snapped, pleased he immediately followed my command, almost running into the bedroom. Even though the three of us were all in this together, I was still the captain. I was in charge and I'd make sure the mating would be perfect for our female.

I smiled at her even though I was still confused by her expression. "Did he do something to you?"

"No. At least, nothing I didn't want him to. But...explain to me why you're wearing this? Is this some sort of tradition?"

I stared at Trish. Had I misread her completely? "It's your tradition, is it not? We read about humans wearing special clothes when trying to seduce each other. Garments with lots of holes to tease. I think Matar called it lacy."

"Lace. Oh my goodness, did you try to make lingerie?" she squealed and covered her mouth with her hands. "That's so adorable!"

Adorable hadn't been what I'd tried to go for - sexy, masculine, seductive had been my intention - but I'd take it.

"Is it what you'd wear on Peritus?"

"Peritus? Ah, you mean Earth, I keep forgetting you have a different name for it. And no, not quite. Usually, it's the woman who wears the lingerie, not the guys."

I looked down at myself in disappointment. I'd thought I'd got this right, but it seemed we'd failed yet again. Chances of passing the IGU course got slimmer with every moment.

"Hey, but you look great," she said and reached out to me, only to pull her hand back just before she touched my chest. "Thank you for trying to make this like what I'm used to. Not that I've ever owned any lingerie-"

"You haven't?" I asked dumbfounded. "But how do you - or have you never-"

"It wasn't a necessity and I didn't have money for anything that wasn't essential," she explained without answering what I'd tried to ask. I supposed it didn't matter if she'd mated before. She was ours now and she'd never return to whatever human male she'd shared her body with.

"We'll make you as much lacy clothes as you want," I promised. "You can show me how they're supposed to look like. But now, would you like to join us in watching a recording of a human couple?"

Her gorgeous eyes widened in surprise. Her pupils were much larger than ours, only leaving a small ring of colour around them, but I thought that only made her more attractive.

"Are we going to watch a movie? A romantic one? That's so sweet. Will there be popcorn?"

"What's that? My translator didn't get that."

"Snacks. Something to eat while watching."

"Why would you want to eat?" I asked. "I was planning to hold hands with you."

And copy some of the things happening on the screen, but it didn't feel right to say that yet. I wanted to surprise her.

"That's very sweet."

I wasn't sure why she kept describing everything as sweet. Did she think we were like confectionary? Humans were strange. Although maybe she expected my seed to be sweet. I had no idea if it was. I'd never asked a female to taste it. Was that something humans did?

The thought of it made my cocks swell further. I was about ready to burst. The anticipation had made me hard and ready for her. I hoped the recording Havel had chosen wasn't too long. I had no patience to sit and watch other people fuck without being inside Trish.

I pressed a button on my comms to open the bedroom door for her, incredibly pleased that I'd remembered that part of seduction etiquette. She gasped as soon as she entered, then began laughing so loud it almost hurt my ears.

"What on Earth have you done to your clothes?" she exclaimed. "Get out of them, that's about the unsexiest thing I've ever seen. You look like you're vagrants."

I didn't know what a vagrant was, but I liked that she wanted us to undress. I got out of my lacy outfit quicker than I thought possible. I followed her into the room, proud of how high my erect cocks were reaching. Maybe she'd let me rut her right away, without the delay of watching that recording.

She turned to look at me, did a strange gurgling sound and swirled around again. "I meant put on something else, not get naked," she squeaked. "I didn't need to see that." She realised the other two had undressed too and squealed again. "Nor that."

I exchanged a look with the other guys. What was the point of getting dressed again if we'd discard our clothes soon after? It seemed like a waste of time.

"Does my physique disappoint you?" I asked.

She slowly turned to me, her eyes fixed on mine, although the concentration on her face made it obvious that she was having to force herself not to look at the rest of my body. "Not exactly. But this isn't right. You abducted me. You shouldn't be naked. You shouldn't be this...big."

She covered her mouth again. I wondered why she kept doing that. I added it to my mental list of questions that I'd eventually ask her. Now wasn't the time.

"I'm slightly above average size," I said proudly. "But if you consider I have two cocks, I am very much above average."

Her face turned redder and redder. "Thanks for letting me know."

"You're welcome. Havel assured me after the probing that you'll be able to take all of us."

"All of you?" she repeated in a high-pitched voice. "At the same time?"

"If you want us to," Havel said smoothly. "We'd love nothing more."

Trish staggered back and sat down on the bed. "This is too much. I should be running, I should be freaked out. Why am I not freaking out?"

"Because we chose you as our female," Matar said, his tail curling around her ankle. She didn't seem to notice or if she did, she didn't mind. "We chose you because we knew you'd be able to cope with this. You're strong, you're beautiful, you're perfect. We've travelled across the galaxy to find you and you were worth every single lightyear."

I nodded, impressed at how eloquent our engineer had suddenly become. Maybe he should try and write some poetry for her after all.

"Every lightyear," I echoed. "Worth it."

"So that means I shouldn't feel bad about...wanting you?" she asked.

My hearts beat so hard it almost hurt. She *wanted* us.

"We want you too," Havel said. "You are all we ever wanted. You don't have to be afraid of your feelings. Everything is new to both you and us. There are no rules. We make our own rules, our own traditions. If we want to wear clothes with holes, that's fine. If we want to walk around naked, that's also fine."

"As long as the Captain agrees," I grumbled, just to make sure she understood that I was still in charge, no matter Havel's pretty words.

"Let's get comfortable," the medic suggested. "The bed is big enough for us all. Do you want to watch that *movie*?"

Trish nodded. "But can you at least slip under the blanket? Seeing you all naked is...well, I'll need time to get used to that."

Nudity was nothing special or embarrassing for Kardarians, but I was aware not all species felt that way. Maybe we could persuade her to stay naked eventually. Drops of golden precum rose to heads of my cocks as I thought of how convenient it would be to have her always available, no need to undress. I could find her whenever I felt the need and plunge into her depths.

Yes, abducting her was the best thing we could have done. And no matter what Professor Katila thought about our probing, it had shown to me that Trish was perfect for us. And that she was willing. She may need a little persuasion, but deep inside she wanted us just as much as we wanted her. It was only her mind telling her to take it slow, while her body betrayed her. Even now, I could smell her arousal.

All three of us joined her in bed and dutifully pulled a blanket over the bottom halves of our bodies.

She didn't ask us to fully cover up all the way to our necks, so hopefully, that was a good sign.

She was squeezed in between me and Havel, with Matar on the medic's right. He'd already had his kiss with her and should, therefore, wait his turn. We hadn't talked about it, but it was proof of how well this crew knew each other. Soon, Trish would be part of us. She'd be our family, gluing us all together. Our mate.

Havel's eyes glazed over as he used his comms to select the recording. The large screen at the other end of the bed flickered on, revealing three humans in a dark room. The lights had been strategically positioned to highlight only parts of their bodies, adding to the mystery and suspense. The two males caressed the female between them, stroking her hair, her body, then one of them kissed her on the lips.

"Ehm, that's not a romance movie," Trish laughed. "Are you watching porn?"

"Yes, this is a pornographic recording," Havel confirmed. "I found it in your planetary database. Is it not to your liking? I have others with just a couple or several females or-"

"You don't usually watch porn on your first date," she explained. "We watch films about two people falling in love. Usually, there's something that stops them coming together but when they finally do, it's even sweeter." She smiled. "Romance isn't all about sex, you know?"

I nodded, proud that I knew that. "Yes, you're right. It's also about other things. Like seduction and wooing and kissing."

For some reason, she rolled her eyes, but she didn't say anything. I reached out to hold her hand. Her fingers were so much thinner than mine and I was worried I might crush her delicate hand. She didn't pull back, not even when Matar took her other hand and lifted it to his mouth. He kissed her thumb, then the other fingers one by one. With each kiss, Trish became redder. Was there a limit to how red her skin could become? I didn't want her to be permanently red like a luovi fruit. I hated those. They were too sweet.

One of the males in the recording went to his knees and pressed his face against the female's arse. His nose sunk in the valley between her cheeks. The camera didn't show what his tongue did but I bet he was tasting her. He wrapped his hands around her thighs and pulled them apart, giving him better access. I took in every detail, committing it to memory. I'd do that with Trish someday. In fact, what was stopping me from tasting her right now?

I let go of her hand and pulled up her dress until I was able to touch her sex. I was too impatient to do anything but plunge a finger into her. She was warm and tight and her inner muscles contracted around my finger as if they were hugging my cocks. Klat. I'd planned to pull out and lick off her liquids, but now that my finger was deep inside her, I couldn't stop. She moaned when I started moving, exploring her insides. This was much better than probing. The probe hadn't been able to tell us what it would feel like to touch the warm, wet skin that led to her womb. I would plant my seed into her. Right now.

I threw back the blanket, my cocks twitching when cold air hit them. Trish moaned, but she didn't protest. On the contrary, her eyes were closed and her lips parted as her breath turned faster and faster. She liked it. I grinned. This was only the beginning.

Something nudged my hand. Matar's tail. Its tip had swollen; something I'd never seen it do. I hadn't realised his tail could change shape. It almost looked like a cock, which instantly turned it into a competition. Still, I wanted to see what would happen, so I pushed my finger to the side, giving the tail space to enter her too.

It pushed against her entry, needing some force to fit. Maybe I should pull away my hand, but I didn't want to leave her. The tip of Matar's tail twisted and turned until it slid in, aided by the liquid leaking from Trish's sex. It shot into her, hard and deep, deeper than my finger could reach. That was unacceptable. I had to match it.

Trish groaned and threw her head from side to side. "More," she moaned. "More."

She didn't have to tell me twice. I finally pulled

out and licked the finger now glistening with her wetness.

Her nipples were hard and pointed, inviting me to suck on them. Havel was faster. He licked them first, one after the other, then wrapped his lips around one and started sucking. The sound of it nearly drove me insane.

If he had her breasts, I'd take her pussy. It was time for Matar's tail to leave. I grabbed it and pulled it out gently for Trish's sake. I didn't want to hurt her in my frenzy to have her for myself. The tail's end turned and pointed at me as if it wanted to protest, but then Matar pulled it to himself and licked it, tasting her. I realised I hadn't done that yet, even though it was why I'd first penetrated her.

I sucked on my finger and her taste exploded on my tongue. I stopped breathing as an overwhelming need took over. I had to be inside her.

My cocks were already covered in the gel that would make it easier to fuck our little human without causing her discomfort. She was full of her own liquid, but I wasn't sure how effective that was. I grabbed her waist and pulled her around until my cocks were pointing at her sex. Havel growled in protest as her breasts were ripped from him, but Trish only moaned, looking at me from half-closed eyes.

"Are you ready to be mated?" I asked her. It felt right to say those words.

"I am," she moaned, barely more than a whisper. "Fuck me."

That was all the encouragement I needed. I positioned my lower cock at her entrance, not wanting to overwhelm her with both at once. I pushed in just a little bit to make sure my gel was working, then when she didn't show any signs of pain, I rammed my cock into her in one hard, confident stroke.

She screamed, her hands gripping the bedsheet, her hips jerking upwards to let me plunge in even deeper. I grabbed her even tighter and fucked her, letting go of all inhibition. I was wild, a predator taking his prey. My upper cock rubbed against her folds, enough to get me close to coming. I usually needed to fist it, touching it from all sides, but this human was far better than my own hands could ever be.

I groaned as I set a fast rhythm, sweat pearling on my back. Havel's mouth was back on her nipples while Matar's tail nudged her lips open until she took him in, sucking him like a cock. I was going to have words with Matar about that tail of his. The engineer was watching without touching himself, but he was hard and there was no doubt he was waiting his turn. We'd all take her today. This first mating was for all of us.

"I'm so close," she gasped. "Just keep-aaaaaaaarrh!"

She threw her head back and let out a scream as her body began to shake, her inner walls fisting my cock. That was my undoing. With a scream that equalled hers, I came, one cock filling her with my seed and the other shooting it all over her belly, creating a beautiful golden pattern. As I watched, it seeped into her skin, staining it like a tattoo. Our mating mark. Now it was time for Havel and Matar to do the same so that every male in the galaxy knew that she was ours.

It was hard to leave her welcoming depths, but as the captain, I had a responsibility to my crew. They were in need of relief and it was their turn.

I pulled out as slowly as I could. This wasn't goodbye; this was just the beginning. I'd get to know every part of her body, inside and out. Maybe again later today. We'd have to discover how often she could be mated with before she needed a break.

I retreated to the end of the bed and leaned against the cool metal wall. I needed a shower, but there was no way I'd miss watching Havel and Matar mark her.

Havel had already taken my place, his single cock ready to enter her.

"Do you want this?" he asked while caressing her breasts. He seemed obsessed with them. Not a surprise, they were stunning.

"Fuck me already, you stupid alien!"

He laughed and did as she'd asked. Trish grabbed

Matar's arm and pulled him closer until his cock was close enough for her to touch. Instead of stroking him like I'd expected, she directed him to her mouth. Oh A'Ta, she was going to swallow him like his tail. More seed spouted from my cocks. This was reaching a new level of mating frenzy. I started rubbing myself, impatient for them to be done with her so I could have another go.

Matar was careful with her, clearly afraid to hurt her, but she grabbed the base of his cock and pulled him into her mouth. He should be glad that she didn't have fangs like Havel. That would have been dangerous. She sucked him, taking him in deep, making choking noises that were almost my undoing. I closed my eyes, touching my cocks, imagining it was her. She was addictive, more so than any drug I'd tried during my wild metamorphosis years.

I only looked up again when Havel roared his release, his blue seed spurting all over her abdomen. Before it could sink into her skin, the liquid turned into single drops forming a circle around the strange indentation on her belly. Only when they were in position did they turn into permanent marks the colour of Havel's skin.

Matar never made it to her pussy. He came moments after Havel, just about managing to pull out of her mouth before shooting his seed on her breasts with a guttural groan. It first accumulated around her nipples, then ran down her mounds leaving beautiful blue stripes like the rays of a burning star.

Spent, he lay down on his back by her side, entwining his fingers with her. Matar's tail lazily curled up on her stomach, right above the bright blue marks. I was about to join them when my comms beeped. Not now. I checked the caller, ready to reject the call, but it was Professor Katila. If she contacted us, it had to be important.

I made sure the video function was switched off before greeting her. My voice was husky still, but hopefully, she wouldn't notice.

"I hope I'm not disturbing?"

I exchanged a look with the guys who grinned at me. "Not at all. What can I do for you?"

"I have looked at your grades and I'm afraid it doesn't look good for you. You've shown promise in some areas of the course, but you've failed several important parts of the abduction process. Even if you perform well in an oral examination, it won't be enough. There is however a way for you to pass the course and gain your certification."

"How?" I asked sharply while Matar gasped. I realised he'd not seen our results yet. Poor guy. Havel started whispering to him and Trish, explaining what had happened.

"First, I will have to talk to your abductee and ask her some questions. If what she says is satisfactory, I will let you know the next step."

I didn't like that she didn't divulge all the information immediately, but she was the teacher and we the students. The authority lay with her.

"Alright. She's with me just now, would you like to talk to her right away?"

Trish blinked tiredly, taken aback. She shook her head, but it was too late.

"Yes, that would be fabulous. You can stay on the line but please don't interrupt."

I felt a little like a child again, being chastised by my elders. I hated that feeling. I was the captain of this klatting ship; I deserved respect.

Matar helped Trish up and let her lean against his chest while Havel offered her a drink. She emptied the entire tumbler in one go, then licked her lips that were stained green from sucking Matar's cock. That colour should fade though; I'd never heard of a mating mark becoming permanent on a female's face. Not that it would make her any less beautiful, but she may not want to walk around with blue stains on her lips and chin for the rest of her life.

"Abductee, please report your state of health," Professor Katila commanded, suddenly sounding reserved and clinical.

"Ehm, I'm well," Trish muttered, shooting me a questioning look. "I was injured back on Earth but when the guys abducted me, they healed all my injuries. Actually, I don't think I've ever felt better."

She grinned at the three of us, clearly referring to the aftereffects of the mating. Our human - no, our mate - seemed to be glowing with joy. Pride filled my heart. I was proud of how she was handling her abduction, proud of having her as my mate.

"Did the abductors explain to you why they abducted you?"

"Yes, they did. I thought I'd already said that when Havel interviewed me for his assignment."

"They explained to you that they wanted you as their mate and breeder?" the Professor asked.

Trish blushed a little. "They did."

"And you weren't scared when you heard that?"

"Of course I was scared. Although, I first thought it was a joke. Then I was scared. Then I realised it may not be as bad as it sounded. Now I think this is the best thing that could have happened to me. I had no one on Earth. Now I have three guys desperate to make me happy."

"Now? Does that mean you've mated?"

Trish looked at me as if looking for reassurance. I nodded encouragingly and she rewarded me with a smile.

"Yes. We have."

"Was the experience satisfactory?"

Our female snorted with amusement. "You could say that."

"Good. I assume that means you're content to

continue the abduction experience without resistance or escape attempts?"

Again, Trish laughed. "Yes, I don't plan to run away from this."

She looked at Havel, then Matar, then me, appraising our naked bodies. I looked down at my cocks, thanking them for being able to pleasure Trish so thoroughly. I wasn't sure if our personalities were enough to keep her with us. We'd failed with the lacy clothes and the recording of the couple. I glanced at the screen where the female was impaled on both men's cocks, unmoving. Havel must have stopped the video at some point. It would make a nice wall decoration, inspiring us for the next mating.

"Excellent. I need you to be fully compliant for the next stage. We are setting up a new course for advanced learners. Only those who've completed the first abduction certifications can take part."

"Does that mean we passed?" Matar interrupted eagerly.

"We will need case studies for the course," the Professor continued, ignoring the engineer's question. "If you agree, we will follow you three as you progress with your abductee. As part of the course, other students will analyse your behaviour to learn from it. This means you will be recorded on camera most days during the experiment. I will give you pointers in what to do and how best to proceed, but in the end, the decisions on what to do with your abductee is up to you. At the end of the course, I will decide whether you get the certification or not."

"Certification for this course or both?" Havel asked.

"I will mark you as passed for this course as soon as you agree to be our case study. I will even raise your grades a little to give you a 'good' rather than a 'passable'. I really think you're the perfect group of individuals to learn from. What do you say?"

I looked first at Matar and Havel, then at Trish. Matar looked angry but gave me a curt nod. Havel was more enthusiastic, clearly ecstatic that we might pass the course after all. Trish showed me her thumbs. I didn't know what that meant, but her smile said enough.

"We say yes," I told the Professor. "We're going to do it."

I reached out and took Trish's hands in mine.

Our abduction adventure wasn't over yet.

The story continues in Alien Abduction for Professionals. *Here's a tiny spoiler: Trish will get a tribitt as a pet!*
Flick the page to see what it looks like...

If you enjoyed this book, please consider leaving a review.

Want more books? Subscribe to my newsletter: https://skyemackinnon.com/newsletter

COULD YOU ABDUCT A HUMAN?

Do you think you've got what it takes to become an alien abductor? Take this test to find out!
skyemackinnon.com/alien-abduction-test

(if you share your results on social media, be sure to tag me)

And if you feel like you've passed this course, you can download a certificate!
hi.switchy.io/AAFBcertificate

THE INTERGALACTIC GUIDE TO HUMANS

Abductions aren't easy - which is exactly why the Intergalactic University offers a range of courses at various levels. Immerse yourself in this strange, comical universe and work on your abduction skills.

Find all books in this series here:

skyemackinnon.com/intergalactic-guide

Alien Abduction for Beginners

Alien Abduction for Professionals

Alien Abduction for Experts

(*reverse harem/why choose trilogy, to be read in order*)

Alien Abduction for Santa

(*fmf standalone*)

Alien Abduction for Pirates

(*mf standalone*)

Alien Abduction for Milkmen

(*mm standalone*)

Alien Abduction for Unicorns

(*mf standalone*)

THE STARLIGHT UNIVERSE

This book is part of the Starlight Universe, an entire galaxy filled with hunky aliens, exotic planets, and the human women ready to find love among the stars.

Starlight Highlanders Mail Order Brides

Alien Highlanders in kilts come to Earth in search of brides... and take them to planet Albya. Three m/f standalones full of humour, action and steamy romance. Part of the Intergalactic Dating Agency.

The Intergalactic Guide to Humans

A humorous take on alien abductions, probing and other shenanigans. One reverse harem trilogy about clueless aliens and the human woman they abducted, followed by several standalone romances with various pairings (m/f, f/m/f and m/m). If you want light entertainment filled with unicorns, fabulous misunderstandings and unusual body parts, this is the series for you.

Starlight Vikings

Set on Earth and on the spaceship Valkyr, this trilogy of m/f standalones is all about hunky alien Vikings in need of females. Part of the Intergalactic Dating Agency.

Starlight Monsters

These aliens are not your usual humanoids... they have claws, fangs, tails, scales, knotty dicks and will growl at you. Interconnected m/f standalones with lots of action, steam and fated mates.

ABOUT THE AUTHOR

Skye MacKinnon is a Scottish romance author who was raised by elves in the mystical Highlands and calls the Loch Ness monster her friend. Her bestselling books weave together romance with action, suspense and whimsical humour, creating page-turners filled with strong heroines, alpha heroes and loveable monsters.

Whether she's writing about aliens in kilts, hunky Vikings or cat shifter assassins, Skye likes to put a new spin on familiar tropes. Some of her heroines don't have to choose, some fall in love with other women, and others get abducted by clueless aliens.

Skye lives with her bossy cat on the west coast of Scotland and uses the dramatic views from her office as an inspiration, no matter whether she writes fantasy, paranormal or science fiction romance. Until she gets abducted by aliens, that is.

Subscribe to her newsletter:

skyemackinnon.com/newsletter

ALSO BY SKYE MACKINNON

Find all of Skye's books on her website, skyemackinnon.com, where you can also order signed paperbacks and swag. Many of her books are available as audiobooks.

PARANORMAL & FANTASY ROMANCE

- **Claiming Her Bears** (post-apocalyptic shifter reverse harem)
- **Daughter of Winter** (fantasy reverse harem)
- **Catnip Assassins** (urban fantasy reverse harem)
- **Infernal Descent** (paranormal reverse harem based on Dante's Inferno, co-written with Bea Paige)
- **Seven Wardens** (fantasy reverse harem co-written with Laura Greenwood)

- **The Lost Siren** (post-apocalyptic, paranormal reverse harem co-written with Liza Street)

SCIENCE FICTION ROMANCE

- **Starlight Highlanders Mail Order Brides** (sci-fi m/f romance, part of the Intergalactic Dating Agency)
- **Starlight Vikings** (sci-fi m/f romance, part of the Intergalactic Dating Agency)
- **Starlight Monsters** (m/f romance)
- **The Intergalactic Guide to Humans** (sci-fi romance with various pairings)
- **Between Rebels** (sci-fi reverse harem set in the Planet Athion shared world)
- **The Mars Diaries** (sci-fi reverse harem)
- **Through the Gates** (dystopian reverse harem co-written with Rebecca Royce)
- **Aliens and Animals** (f/f sci-fi romance co-written with Arizona Tape)

OTHER SERIES

- **Academy of Time** (time travel academy standalones, reverse harem and m/f)
- **Defiance** (contemporary reverse harem with a hint of thriller/suspense)

STANDALONES

- Song of Souls – m/f fantasy romance, fairy tale retelling
- Wings of Time and Fate - YA fantasy
- Their Hybrid – steampunk reverse harem
- Partridge in the P.E.A.R. - sci-fi reverse harem co-written with Arizona Tape
- Highland Butterflies – lesbian romance

BOX SETS

- Daggers & Destiny – a Skye MacKinnon starter library
- Stars & Seduction - a Sci-Fi Romance starter library

www.ingramcontent.com/pod-product-compliance
Ingram Content Group UK Ltd.
Pitfield, Milton Keynes, MK11 3LW, UK
UKHW040008200726
13854UKWH00001B/99

9 798201 342272